Speechless

by

Kate Darbishire

Cover Design by Peter Haillay

DEDICATION

To my dear Katie and to all those children
who have problems with mobility and
communication and face the world with
cheerfulness, valiance and determination.
You teach me every day to be more human.

Chapter 1

"We're having a baby."

That's what she said. Just like that. As though it was the most natural, normal thing in the world. But nothing would ever be normal in this family.

"Isn't that exciting?"

It all made sense now – the green face, rushing off to the loo in the middle of things, looking tired all the time.

"Do you know what I'm saying, Harriet? We're going to have a new baby." Mum crossed her arms in front of her, using her right hand to mimic the shape of a baby's head. The Makaton sign for baby.

I sighed – of course I knew what she was saying – and signed back... 'baby'.

I should explain. I've got Cerebral Palsy and part of that means talking is hard for me. Well, talking isn't so hard – I know what I want to say – it's getting people to understand me is the hard part. I can't be bothered with it most of the time. Signing is just easier – if you're saying something simple and if the person you're talking to knows how to do it.

"I thought you'd be pleased," said Mum, her eyes all soppy, searching into mine as though she was begging me to understand and be happy for her.

Unable to hold her gaze I glared down at my feet which had their usual early morning purple hue. Always cold, my legs, no matter *how* many blankets Mum put on the bed. Why would I be pleased? A baby was a horrible thought. Who would look after me when there was an ultra-cute-vomit-monster, an impostor, vying for attention? And give it a year and it would be chatting away and crawling around the house as if it owned the place, making me look even more of a thicko than I do already.

"Come on... don't look so worried," said Mum, stroking my face as though she could *make* me smile. Really, just because I'm in a wheelchair it doesn't mean I need to be treated like some senile old granny. "Dad's just got a few more contracts to tie up at work and then we'll have him around most of the time. With both of us here we can easily manage you and a new baby." It sounded as though she was trying to convince herself more than me. She went back to doing up the buttons of my blouse.

"Well, I don't know about you, but I hope it's a little girl... you'll have to help me find pretty dresses and things for her. It'll be fun."

I shrugged and nodded half-heartedly. It was a bit late to ask my opinion now, wasn't it? It sounded like the deed was already done. Fait accompli.

"There, you look quite respectable," said Mum shaking my tie into place. "We'll just do your hair... Oh bother! I left your brush in the kitchen. Back in a mo..."

Pushing the round black knob on the arm of my wheelchair forward I steered my way over to the desk and glanced crossly into the mirror which hung above it. I didn't know about having a baby around, but it would be good if Dad wasn't away on business so much. I made a face then smiled my best smile at my reflection. Even trying my hardest the right side of my face contorted into a grimace before the left side had a chance to catch up. I was lopsided, ghoulish. I often think I look like a witch. Hazel eyes peer dully from my heavy lids which are framed by perfect, tidy eyebrows, made for a face that works. Actually, my eyebrows are good, definitely Mum's side of the family – I have 'normal' eyebrows. I can put that on my resume – 'witch-like kid with normal eyebrows'. I brushed my hand through my hair and my fingers caught in the tangles which made me look even more wild and hag-like.

If only I really was a witch, perhaps I could undo some of the bad spells thrown at me by this stinking lottery of life.

The hairbrush scratching through my dreadlocks brought me crashing back to reality and Mum scraped my hair into plaits so tight I knew they would drag on my head all day. Doesn't Mum realise no-one wears plaits at secondary school?

"There we go, Harriet, we're done," said Mum snapping the last band into place. "Now, I haven't told your brother about the baby yet. I wanted you to be the first to know – a secret girlie thing, you know?"

I watched mum's face in the mirror and saw the smile slowly fade.

"Actually, we *are* a little bit worried after everything that went wrong last time..." Honestly, sometimes I wonder if Mum is like everyone else, assuming that I don't understand just because I don't speak much. She turned red though and started to look all flustered. "Sorry... I didn't mean it to sound like that. Anyway, don't say anything to Jake yet, OK?"

I shook my head and made a face that I hoped said: *I won't, Mum.*

"OK, you get sorted. I'll call you when the minibus comes."

Her walk was effortless and elegant as she left my bedroom. Packing my schoolbag with the books for Monday's lessons I wondered if she ever thought about how lucky she was. Just being able to walk.

The mirror caught my attention again and a familiar tune wandered into my head. Ever since I first heard this song, it has stuck in my mind – the constant theme tune of my life:

'I cannot hide from what I see,
A mirror never shows the real me.
Inside I laugh, inside I crave,
Inside I cry, inside I'm brave,
I am not what you believe.
Inside – I am me.'

Chapter 2

The driver who takes me to and from school is called Sam. He's so tall and gangly it's like his smooth dark skin is stretched over thin hard chicken-wire muscles like the animal models we made in art last term. I made a cat and painted it black. Secretly I called it Sam.

Sam talks to me as if I'm an ordinary child – no, better than that – he speaks to me like I'm an adult and he breaks all the rules and asks questions I can answer easily. People are always being told to use 'open' questions when they are talking to me so that I have to use my voice to answer. They're meant to say things like: 'What lessons have you got today?' I hate it. Sam is different.

The door of the minibus slammed shut behind me and Sam ambled round and leapt up into the front seat.

"Brakes on?" he said, craning his neck to look at me.

I gave him the thumbs up sign.

Sam winked and turned back to the front.

"Did you go horse riding this weekend?" he asked starting up the minibus and pulling out into the street.

Yes. I nodded.

"Fun?"

I screwed up my face and made fists of my hands, pretending to shake.

Sam was watching in the rear-view mirror.

"Cold, was it?" he laughed.

Yes.

"Mmm... not so good then."

Sam hummed and fiddled with the radio, looking for the jazz channel we always listened to and I was busy imagining how different my life would soon be if Mum really did have a baby. The conversation was so surreal and unexpected I was starting to think I had made it up.

"Here, Harry, I've got something to tell you."

I've always liked the way Sam calls me Harry. No one else in the world calls me Harry.

"I've got a date tonight!"

I grinned. As far as I knew, he had never had a girlfriend and he was obviously excited.

"The thing is, I don't know whether to take her to the cinema... it's quite a violent film... what's that, Harry?"

I shook my head.

"Nah. Reckon you're right. Perhaps we should just go to the pub."

He shouldn't take her anywhere too rough. I wondered what sort of place he usually went to – would all his friends be there gawping at her? We had stopped at the traffic lights by the park, almost there.

"What is it?" Sam studied my face in the mirror. "You mean somewhere quiet?"

Sam was brilliant. He could read me like a book. I nodded with my big wonky smile all over my face. I do like being around Sam. It's amazing – he actually makes talking seem like a doddle.

We pulled up outside the school and Sam went to the back of the minibus to lower the ramp. I gazed up at Milton Comp. I had been here for nearly two terms now, but the sight of the hundred huge windows staring down at me still gave me butterflies.

"Come on, sleepy-head," called Sam. "I know you'd rather come with me to the Centre and get the oldies for their day trip. But school awaits!"

I turned the wheelchair to see Sam's lanky body doubled over as he peered in at me, eyes twinkling from his thin face. Funny how a man who is over six feet tall never seems to look down at me.

Jerking the chair to the top of the ramp, I rolled down as slowly as possible, my feet diving first. I loathed that ramp. At the bottom, Sam thrust out his hand.

"High five!" he demanded.

I couldn't help smiling as I reached up to slap his hand.

"Off you go, Harry. Knock-em dead."

Chapter 3

I watched the stream of kids piling past me, pulling their coats round them with their heads bent to the wind. Everyone had that Monday-morning-glum look. The calls of "A'right, mate?" were answered with grunts and, "Can't wait to get inside. It's freezing". In my chair, with my bag on my lap, you could say I was partly sheltered from the cold. I could hear Mum's voice in my head: *Thank God for small mercies*. Shows how much Mum knows. I'd need about six duvets over my legs to keep out the pain that whistles into my knees when it's windy.

It is always awkward to join this anonymous sea of waists and chests plodding into school. The best way is to look up and catch someone's eye, so they'll let you in. But I hate drawing attention to myself like that and I hate people looking at me whatever the reason. I'd rather wait for a space and try and slip in amongst them unnoticed. But doing this, trying to get the timing right, always makes me anxious. There was a gap coming up after one of the Year 10 boys. I sort of knew him. It was Cameron, from my brother Jake's class. He came over for a sleepover once, years ago, and even back then he was a bit of a show-off. Today his hair was stuck up in thick greasy spikes and he was preening it as he strode past. I pushed the knob of my motorised chair and jerked forward. Much too fast. Before I knew it, I had collided with Cameron's legs. I knocked him off balance and he nearly fell into my lap! He grabbed the arm of my chair trying to balance himself, his face suddenly right next to mine. I could smell his toothpaste.

"You stupid cow! Watch where you're going," he snarled, glaring at me.

Sorry! I was mortified.

Cameron gave me such a nasty look I wished I could just evaporate into thin air. Then he stormed off into school.

Inside the main entrance, beside the wonky pile of granite blocks drizzled in a trickle of water, one of my classmates was waiting for me as usual. It was Charlotte, slim and blonde, her uniform just perfect. I knew she didn't want to be there, but she'd been given the job of getting 'the cripple' to her lessons this month. Popular and chatty, Charlotte was going to resent having to shepherd me around the school throughout March because it meant she couldn't be with her own friends.

"Hi, Harriet." She smiled her sweet fake smile. "Good weekend?"

10

I tried to make my face express my answer, screwing up my nose and smiling faintly. I wished I could be like Charlotte; loads of mates round me just because I was clever and pretty.

We turned into the corridor, dark, away from the brightness of the main entrance with its tacky water feature.

"Well, Harriet. What did you get up to?"

I ignored her. I couldn't answer *that* question with a yes or no.

"Go on... tell me." Charlotte stepped in front of the wheelchair forcing me to stop suddenly – I didn't want a repeat of the Cameron incident. Not knowing what to do I just gazed at her stupidly, feeling awkward, noticing the perfect symmetry of her clear, pale face.

"Sorry." Charlotte looked embarrassed. "But I would like to know."

I looked down at my stupid purple bag with the word 'princess' on it in fluffy white lettering. Mum got me it for Christmas, but everyone else had black Adidas bags.

"Harriet?" Charlotte's presence towered over me, demanding an answer.

As well as going horse riding, Dad had actually managed to keep Sunday free and we'd been ten-pin bowling. And wouldn't it be lovely to tell someone the new secret trapped inside me like a grain of sand inside an oyster? To be able to tell someone that my mum was going to have a baby! When Mairead told everyone last term that her mum was pregnant, all the girls crowded around her, really excited. Everyone liked Mairead now. But telling Charlotte? Charlotte probably didn't even know the sign for baby and I just didn't speak to people at school. Not anymore. It was different at St. John's, my primary school. There I knew everyone. They had been used to me since Reception with Mrs Thomas.

"Come on, Harriet. Alice says you can speak."

Well, Alice would. And I could imagine what else Alice would have said too. Alice was the one girl at St. John's who really couldn't stand me. How come she was the only girl from my primary school who had been put into my form at Milton Comp? Like a sick joke.

"Please, Harriet. Can't you tell me what you did at the weekend?" Charlotte had enormous blue eyes like a little grey kitten. She crouched down next to the chair and looked earnestly into my face making me feel even more uncomfortable.

Was it a trick? If I said anything would Charlotte go and tell everyone – sneering and laughing behind my back? I couldn't tell. On the spur of the moment, I decided what to do.

"No. Please," I said. What I hoped would be a tiny whisper came out like sandpaper scratching a wall. My voice sounded worse than ever.

Charlotte's mouth dropped open and her eyes sparkled (was that malice?). She stood up.

"OK, Harriet. Maybe later?"

Following Charlotte along the corridor, I felt as though an iron fist was gripping my intestines. This was it. Charlotte was going to hold the classroom door open for me because she had to. Then she was going to run in, boasting to everyone that she'd made me talk. Everyone would crowd round the chair, teasing me, trying to make me talk some more. Well, I wouldn't. Ever again.

"Harriet?"

I looked up reluctantly as I passed Charlotte into the form room.

"Don't look so worried."

Get lost.

I wished my desk was further away from Charlotte and her cronies. My ears were hot and pounding and everyone was looking at me. I stroked the soft fluffy lettering on my bag, letting it tickle my fingers. If I was a real princess, I would be just... sublime... straight and tall and pretty. I'd have little pointy heels on my shoes (with gold tips) and long dark hair cascading down my shoulders, shimmering and sleek. Because everyone knows that princesses are always perfect. Everyone would be my friend.

13

"Harriet Harris?"

"She's here, Miss."

"Ah, Harriet, don't forget the physiotherapist is coming to see you in your P.E. lesson. OK? During your P.E. lesson this morning." Miss Jenkins' voice was laced with honey and she spoke loud and slow, as though she didn't expect me to understand.

Miss Jenkins, my form teacher, was a stout woman who wore brown pleated skirts. Her hair was pulled back in a tight bun, exposing large masculine ears and steely grey eyes which stood out on stalks when she got annoyed. Not only did Miss Jenkins insist on speaking to me like I was stupid, I was quite sure that she simply didn't like me and thought I had no right to be at a normal school.

Looking around the class I decided that if Charlotte had told her friends, the news hadn't spread yet. Everything looked the same as usual. Greg was playing with his ruler, flicking it over the side of the table so that it buzzed.

"Stop that, Gregory," sniped Miss Jenkins.

There was a titter around the room. Greg hated to be called Gregory. Flushing angrily, he stowed his ruler in his bag. I stole a look over at Charlotte's table where Alice, Thea and Codey were all whispering and giggling. Charlotte, however, was looking directly at me.

14

The bell rang for first lesson. French. The French class was upstairs which meant going all the way back down the corridor to the lift. With Charlotte. Great.

"Ready?"

I nodded without looking up at Charlotte, who stood with Thea at the doorway. Thea nudged Charlotte and whispered something in her ear. They both laughed and Thea tossed her dark bob and danced up the stairs to catch up with Alice and Codey.

In the lift, Charlotte pressed the button for the first floor.

"I'm sorry, Harriet. I didn't mean to upset you."

Charlotte's face looked the picture of innocence. Maybe she was just being nice. But then, why were the others all laughing at me? I shrugged and gave a weak smile.

It's OK-ish. Just don't expect me to speak to you again.

Chapter 4

From my seat, next to the window in the French room, I could see Mme Lefage hurrying along the walkway between the main building and the Science block. Late as usual. A gust of wind off the moors to the North took the pile of papers from her arms and sent them whirling and flapping back along the path like large, petulant snowflakes. Mme Lefage teetered on her heels and struggled as though the wind might also snap her stick-insect body in two, then stormed after the papers hampered by her tight black skirt.

Mrs Alcott, my Learning Support Assistant sat permanently on my right during lessons, ready to help me with my work. I touched her neat, painted fingers which sat patiently on the table and pointed out of the window.

"I'll go and give her a hand," said Mrs Alcott. "I'll be back in a minute."

My LSA at St. John's was called Kim, round and chatty and always one step behind the teacher, rushing out mid-lesson to get worksheets she'd left in the staff-room. Mrs

Alcott is like hyper organised and efficient. She's got a job to do and I'm just part of it.

The class was getting restless. Greg had discovered a new game with his ruler, biting bits off his rubber and hurling them over the table at Juliette who sat on our table to get extra help with her English from Mrs Alcott. Juliette wasn't stupid at all: she was French.

"*Imbicile*," Juliette hissed venomously picking up her bag and moving to a spare seat on the other side of the classroom. French was a doddle for her anyway.

Greg and his side-kick, Trescott, laughed.

"Here go, Tubs," sneered Greg, still enjoying his game. He angled his ruler, loaded with a new fragment of rubber and narrowly missed Tim's head.

"Aw!" laughed Trescott. "How could you miss a target that big? Have another go."

Tim was large, to say the least and prone to flatulence. His biggest problem seemed to be his parents, who allowed him to stuff his lunchbox with Mars bars and Coke, so that now, aged 11, he had puffed out to the size of a baby hippopotamus.

"Leave me alone," whined Tim as he fished a tiny missile out of his thick fair hair.

Across the room, Charlotte and her cronies were draped over Will's and Michael's table, playing with their hair and simpering girlishly.

"Get the cripple," said Trescott.

Here we go! I did my best to ignore them.

At last, Mme Lefage arrived, cheeks dappled pink. She shouted out commands in French which obviously meant "Shut up and settle down!" Mrs Alcott followed her into the room and closing the door she came back to my side like an obedient boomerang. The class became subdued and everyone got out their pens, their faces glazed over, trying to concentrate on the lesson ahead – or pretending to.

I had no idea what the stick-insect was rambling on about now, but from the expressions of those around me, at least in French lessons, I wasn't the only one who was confused. Mrs Alcott came to my rescue by producing a specially prepared worksheet which meant I didn't have to do so much copying out. It seemed all we had to do was match French food words to English ones. The room was quiet, with everyone hunkered over their work.

"Cabbage," said Greg giving me a spiteful look. "*Chou!*"

"You've been asked to work in silence," snapped Mrs Alcott.

After French, Charlotte took me back down in the lift to the form room.

"You OK?" asked Charlotte.

Yes, I nodded. Sort of. Perhaps Charlotte was all right after all. We had been at Milton Comp for over six months now and each

18

month a different person had taken me to my lessons. Until now, everyone had seemed too stuck up or too awkward to try and talk to me and I had assumed Charlotte would be the same – after all, Charlotte was one of the most confident and well-liked girls in the class. She wouldn't want to be associated with someone like me... would she?

I took refuge in the toilet during break. Fortunately, there was a large disabled toilet near the form room. It had a big button beside the door which opened it automatically, saving me the embarrassment of having to be taken by Mrs Alcott and giving me a place of sanctuary all to myself.

After break, Mrs Alcott took me to the empty room beside the fitness suite while the others had their P.E. lesson.

"Thank you, Viv," said Molly, the physiotherapist, as Mrs Alcott held open the heavy door.

"See you later," she said and disappeared.

"Right then, Miss. How're you?"

I smiled.

Molly waited, her pale eyes expected a reply.

"OK," I said at last.

"Isn't your mum coming?"

I shrugged.

Molly waited again.

"Don't know," my disused voice croaked. I wish she wouldn't do this.

"OK then. Perhaps she forgot. Let's see what you can do today. I'd like you to stand up." Her voice rose at the end of the sentence as if it was a question, but really it was an order.

I put the brakes on my chair and Molly crouched down to swing the footplates out of the way.

"Now, make sure your feet are straight before you get up."

The firm pressure of Molly's hands anchored my feet to the floor so that they didn't slip and pushed my heels down as they had a habit of lifting off the ground.

"OK then," said Molly getting up. "Hold onto my hands... come on, back straight."

Almost as tall as Molly now, I watched a strand of grey hair fall against her cheek.

"Bottom in."

I did my best. It was a shame Mum wasn't here. She and Molly always got chatting and Molly was somehow easier to satisfy.

"OK, sit down. I'll have a look at your feet. No! Don't just flop down. You'll hurt yourself like that. Stand up and do it again."

I heaved myself back up and then tried to sit down more gently. It was hard to concentrate on anything today. I kept thinking about the baby. Would everything be all right? Or was that baby curled up all innocent inside Mum's belly but actually growing crooked and crippled like me? What would happen then? Even with Dad around it would be too much to have two 'cabbages' in the house.

"Hey! Dreamer! I asked you to stand up again."

Molly had taken off my ugly hospital-issue Velcroed boots and was stroking and stretching my feet. She released them and stood up to watch me get out of my chair again. My toes pushed into the hard nylon carpet and I pressed my hands down on the arms of the chair. I could tell my heels weren't on the floor.

"No. Right, sit back down and show me how you're getting on with the exercises."

Losing my balance, I crashed back into the chair, groaning.

"Come on. Show me how you can bring your feet to ninety degrees. Right foot first."

My knees jerked inwards as I concentrated. I could feel my toes co-operating, but I knew my ankle was still pointing obstinately to the floor, stupid and twisted.

"Oh dear. Are you any better with the left foot? Has Mum been doing the stretches with you?"

No, Mum hadn't. Not for quite a while. She'd been looking sick and agitated for weeks and her back had been hurting, so she didn't want to get on the floor, especially in the mornings.

Molly tutted. "We'll have to think about doing serial plasters again."

Serial plasters were a nightmare. Every week for six weeks, I would have to go to the hospital and have my legs put into plaster casts, which forced my feet into a 'normal' right angle to my legs. I couldn't see the point: it wasn't as if I'd ever be able to walk. The plaster tickled and itched my feet all week, like red ants running up and down, but I couldn't scratch them. My ankles ached with the constant pressure and everyone gave me sad looks and said, "What have you done to yourself?" or, "Ahh! Have you broken both your legs, dear?" as if to say, "How could you be so careless?" The only good thing was getting a morning off school every week to have the plasters changed.

"All right, Harriet," said Molly when Mrs Alcott came to collect me. "I'll be in touch with your Mum and I'll see you in three weeks... Harriet?" she demanded.

"OK," I replied. I knew I had to speak when Molly was in this kind of mood.

"Viv, does Harriet speak to you much?"

"Well... not really," said Mrs Alcott, obviously having to think about it. She was so used to all the signing and miming that she didn't notice that I almost never used my voice.

"Actually, Viv, it's really important – she can speak, if you insist on it. Can't you, Harriet?"

"Yes," I said reluctantly. *Great, just what I need. Hassle from Mrs Alcott as well. Thanks Molly.*

Chapter 5

Sam had a car in the evenings instead of the minibus. This was good for me because it meant that I could sit up in front, but it was a pain for Sam because he had to struggle getting the chair into the boot. Sam seemed twitchy tonight about his date with Evette. He wittered on, trying to gear himself up. I was only half listening.

The car pulled into Apricot Avenue, the small estate of dormer bungalows where we had lived for the last three years. Hardly any young families lived in the area: it was mostly retired couples. They pottered about in their gardens armed with shears and secateurs, they took their lap dogs out, clutched under their arms, and they congregated in white-haired huddles to catch up on the neighbourhood gossip.

The road took a sweeping left turn and number 32 came into view. Straightaway I saw that things were not right. First, Mum's car wasn't in its usual spot on the drive, next to the jumble of ragged looking wallflowers and the overgrown lawn. Mum was always home when I got back from school. Maybe the car was at the garage...

Second, and even more ominously, in place of Mum's Mitsubishi was a pretentious purple Honda Goldwing. It belonged to Dad's stepfather, Alan. I was always infuriated that my grandmother, Gloria, seemed to think more of her husband's hideous motorbike than she did of her own grandchildren (Jake and I weren't allowed to call her by any name which specified our relationship with her – even Dad has always called her by her first name). Never before had I found Gloria standing at the door of number 32 Apricot Avenue when I came home from school. Yet here she was in her tight leather trousers and a flouncy flamingo coloured blouse, topped with Mum's brand-new apron covered in green dinosaurs.

We hardly ever saw Dad's parents. Gloria's house was spotless and there was no wheelchair access – she was quite firm about that. But it was just an excuse for us not to visit. And I don't think Mum even noticed the way that Gloria seemed to sniff the air whenever I was near her as though I somehow smelt of cat pee.

So, what on earth was this woman doing on the doorstep, looking as though she was preparing tea for the family?

Gloria's mouth was set in a thin, fixed smile. Her eyes bulged and her forehead was furrowed. She had the look of a rabbit in violent pink lipstick, caught in the car headlights.

"Bloomin' Nora! Who's that?" Sam asked, sounding shocked. "Is she your grandmother?"

I wrinkled my nose and nodded. I think Sam got the message.

"Poor you," he said, which made me smile a bit.

"You weren't expecting her, were you? You'll want to find out what's going on. I'll hurry up with the chair."

Gloria approached slowly, looking frankly terrified, as Sam manoeuvred me into the chair.

The curtains twitched next door at number 30. It looked as though Mrs Turner had been watching out. Mrs Turner was an interfering old warthog. Fat, with short wiry bristles of patchy grey hair who came over most mornings for 'a nice cuppa tea and a chat', informing Mum of the way children were brought up in her day (not that she had any children of her own) and Mum was too polite to tell her where to go.

I twisted in my chair to wave a reluctant farewell to Sam and watched Gloria take control of the wheelchair, looking extremely uncertain of what she was doing. Thinking about it I could never remember having been handled in any way by my grandmother. We were both nervous.

"Tar rah!" called Sam, gambolling back to the car and leaving us together like two familiar strangers.

Chapter 6

The phone was ringing as we went into the house. Gloria pushed the chair up towards the cloakroom door in the hall so that she had enough room to shut the front door, then she skipped off into the kitchen to answer the phone.

"Oh, Cynthia, darling, yes, thank you for returning my call."

Crikey, she sounds like she's speaking to the Queen.

"Yes, well, I was apparently the only person who could come at such short notice... yes, sorry Sweetie, I shall have to cancel the gym this evening..."

She's 65 for heaven's sake. What is she doing going to the gym at her age anyway? The idea of my peroxide blonde grandmother pumping iron at the gym made me stifle a giggle. I decided to go to my bedroom and put on the TV. It didn't look as though there was any point hoping for the cocoa and chocolate biscuit I usually had with Mum after school while we waited for Jake to get back. But Sam never remembered to switch the wheelchair onto automatic and I can't reach the button myself because it's at the back of the chair. Stupid design. I was marooned here, in the hall, my feet jammed up against the cloakroom door. If Mum was there, I'd have called her back to sort the chair out but when people don't know me, or know the strange unearthly drone of my voice, I just won't speak. They end up getting confused and frustrated when they can't understand me. It's so embarrassing. I decided to listen in to Gloria's telephone conversation instead.

"I shall have to re-arrange my hair appointment tomorrow. I can't see Liz being allowed out of hospital before Wednesday... Yes, it doesn't look too good... We might have to stay the night, but Anthony will have to come home and see to the children, no matter how ill Liz is."

Mum was ill! She wasn't coming home tonight... but I needed her! It must be the baby. Why hadn't I at least pretended to be happy when Mum told me about it? She had enough to worry about.

"...Can you believe it – I broke my nail, and with the party on Wednesday! Oh! I'm sure Liz will be out by then. Well I hope so... no, I'm not really cut out for it... yes – the bike convention – and Alan and I had planned to make a long weekend of it – exactly... I don't see why it comes down to me. That's right. I'm no good at all with... with the girl..."

Just at that moment the toilet flushed and instead of the silence that had been behind the cloakroom door there was the stumble and thump of someone washing their hands in the sink, knocking the plastic mug onto the floor.

Then the doorknob turned, and the door began to open with some speed – and crashed into my footplate – and my cringing toes. The sound of a body thumping into the door echoed around the house and a shudder reverberated through the wheelchair making me cry out, a shocked, eerie sound, even to my own ears. Alan's voice thundered through the door in a mouthful of curses.

"What the hell is going on, Gloria? I've banged my blooming head. Get here now!"

Gloria abandoned the phone, which bounced on the end of its cord, ricocheting off the fridge. She rushed into the hall, waving her arms about and glaring at me as if I was to blame for all the confusion.

"Alan, baby... I'm sorry. The phone went and I left the chair in the way. I forgot you were in there. My darling! Are you OK?" She flung me away from the door and rushed to rescue her husband.

"Come, come. Let me get you an ice pack. Oh, my love!"

"For Goodness sake, Gloria – you can't leave the child in front of doors," said Alan, resisting his wife's attempts to usher him into the kitchen and dodging past her to retrieve me from behind the front door.

"You OK there?" he asked.

I smiled my lopsided smile. It was so embarrassing to have been the cause of such a scene. Alan pushed me into the sitting room.

"OK, love. You can come and watch telly with me." He ruffled my hair and his scratchy, lined face contorted into a friendly wink.

Gloria had rushed off, tapping up and down the kitchen floor in her pink kitten heels. She could be heard hastily finishing her conversation with Cynthia Darling and then trawling impatiently through the freezer.

The click of Gloria's shoes approached, and she called out as she came into the living room, "There wasn't an icepack, can you believe it? And with children in the house, too! Anyway, here's some 'diced vegetables'," she said with some disdain. "They'll have to do."

"I'm fine, Gloria. Don't fuss."

"Be quiet and hold these against your head or you'll have a terrible bruise."

"Yes, ma'am," he mouthed at Gloria's back as she hurried off to the kitchen.

"I need to get this pie in the oven..."

Alan mimed shooing her out of the room and raised his eyebrows, grinning at his own joke. He brushed his tobacco stained fingers through his wavy grey, shoulder-length hair, adjusted the cravat he always wore around his neck and picked up the remote control, flicking on BBC2. Darts. He looked satisfied.

Great. There was no way I could escape – my chair was still locked on manual and anyway it would be rude to leave now, when Alan was trying so hard to be nice.

My mind began to drift. I was Tinkerbell and whizzed out of the open window and back towards town, heading for the hospital. The revolving door of St Mary's Infirmary was too scary and prevented me flying in.

I flew around the building, looking in at all the windows until at last, I saw Mum who was lying in bed with her eyes closed, either asleep or unconscious. The bed sheets were soaked in blood and there were drips feeding into her arms. She was hooked up to a monitor which measured the beep, beep of her heart; and a machine was breathing for her. Dad was sitting beside the bed, holding mum's hand and Jake sat by the window, crying. He looked out of the window and stood up. I was unsure if I had been seen or not. Jake drew the curtain, blocking my view.

No, I thought, coming to with a start. *It can't be as bad as all that.*

Chapter 7

Sometime later, I heard the key in the front door.

"What's going on?" Jake called. "Where's Mum?"

Gloria's heels clicked into the hall.

"Hello, dear. Now, let me take your coat. It's nice and warm in here with the heating. Come on into the kitchen. Would you like some cocoa?"

"Yes, OK, Gloria. Where's Mum?"

"She's just a bit poorly, darling."

"But where is she? Will she be home soon?"

"Would you like a cookie?"

"Yes, please. Is Harriet here?"

"In the sitting room."

Jake poked his head round the door.

"Hi, Alan."

"Right there, mate. How are you, chum?" But he didn't expect an answer.

My chair was parked beside the new white sofa and Jake perched himself next to me, on its arm.

"What's going on? I can't get anything out of Gloria," he whispered.

We glanced over at Alan, in Dad's chair, engulfed in a cloud of cigarette smoke like the mist around a church gargoyle. But he seemed transfixed by Johnny Freeman's arm gliding slowly back and forth, aiming at the bullseye.

"Hospital!" I tried to keep my stupid unpredictable voice as quiet as possible.

"Who Mum? What's wrong with her?" Jake looked as worried as I felt.

I don't know. I wondered about telling him Mum was pregnant but decided it was too complicated. And anyway, Mum had told me not to say anything.

"You don't know? Well Gloria must know," he said, getting up to leave.

"Ake," I always found my 'j's very difficult.

Jake turned, almost tripping over his size 11s, which had grown faster than the rest of his body.

"Chair?" I signalled for Jake to put the chair on auto.

Jake gave me a look of disbelief.

Yeh! Gloria's rubbish, isn't she?

Jake switched the button at the back of the chair so that I could drive myself and I followed him into the kitchen.

"Gloria, why's Mum in hospital?"

"I... well... I don't know, dear." She buried her head in the biscuit cupboard. Whatever she did know she obviously wasn't going to tell us. "Your father just called and asked me to be here for you coming home. I'm sure he'll tell us what's happened when he gets back..."

Jake looked at me with the palms of his hands raised to the ceiling. *I give up on her,* his manner suggested. He hoisted himself onto the work surface next to the sink.

"Have you had some cocoa, Harriet?" he asked, automatically cupping his hand into the Makaton sign for drink.

No.

"Oh, er... sorry, I've been a bit busy. We'll get some on now for her." Gloria measured out a second cup of milk and poured it in the pan. "So, Jakie, what have you been doing at school? Have you got any homework you need help with?"

Jake rolled his eyes behind Gloria's back.

"It's OK. I'll take my drink and biscuits up to my room and get on with it."

"All right, love. Just you let me know if you need any help, won't you? I don't suppose Harriet gets homework, does she? Poor little thing."

Jake gave me a questioning look.

No, I shook my head at him. My homework would wait until Mum came back.

Gloria made a big fuss about the silly cocoa, frothing it up and everything. She even found some mini marshmallows to put on top so that I had to admit it looked yummy as Gloria put the steaming mugs on the table.

"Oh, does Harriet need some extra milk to cool it down?"

"No, she'll be fine," said Jake. Swinging his legs, he jumped down from the worktop.

Jake took four chocolate biscuits from the fancy floral plate Gloria had found hidden away somewhere in the cupboard and disappeared upstairs to his bedroom.

I picked up my biscuits and cocoa and made to take them to my room.

"No, no, dear. You'd better sit up to the table. Have a plate and try not to make a mess." Gloria looked at me as though trying to ascertain whether I was safe eating without a bib.

I did as I was told, but it didn't taste so good now. Gloria ignored me and carried on making the dinner. It looked as though she was trying to make pastry. She had cut some butter into squares and put it into the big glass mixing bowl. The flour was measured out on the scales and Gloria had shaken a pinch of salt on top of it. Now she was on her hands and knees, like a skinny rat, searching through all the cupboards. I didn't care. If Gloria didn't think it was worth asking me where the sieve was then I couldn't be bothered to show her that Mum hung it on a hook at the end of the cupboards.

Chapter 8

We moved into this house when I got my new wheelchair. I needed more space to get about and I was getting too heavy to be lifted up and down the stairs. It's great, having an electric wheelchair gives me so much more freedom – and I got to have the biggest bedroom. Mum and Dad and Jake had the two upstairs bedrooms. I hardly ever went up there – in fact it had been nearly a year since I had. It was on Mother's Day. Jake had made poached egg and a cafetière of coffee while I arranged some tulips in a vase and wrapped up a little fish wind-chime which now hung above the kitchen table and jangled merrily whenever the side door opened. Dad was away, as usual, so it was just the three of us. Getting up the stairs was a bit of a palaver. I sat on my bum on the bottom step, trying to drag myself up backwards. But there was just no way! In the end, Jake left the tray on the landing, outside the shower room, and had to come back down the stairs to help. He just about managed to piggyback me, but all the banging about, the laughing and the shushing, woke Mum up and ruined the surprise.

Next to my bathroom downstairs was the spare room which doubled as an office. It was always dark, because the only window faced the Warthog's bungalow next door. But Mum was good with colour. She had painted it a warm burgundy and hung thick velvet curtains, which made it feel cosy. I clicked on the light switch which like all the others downstairs had been moved to hand-height-for-wheelchair-users.

This was not a room I went into very often. I was being nosy because I wanted to see if Gloria really was staying the night. And there, staring gormlessly from the bed like a pair of sightless black mummies were two motorcycle helmets and matching leather biking suits. On the floor was a leopard-skin overnight bag. I wished I could set fire to it with my eyes.

Above the bed was a black and white photo of me and Jake with Mum and Dad. It had been taken about five years earlier when I was still quite small, on a day trip to Wookey Hole. Dad had carried me into the dripping cave which glowed eerily with amber and green lights. I can still clearly remember the famous witch, looming large and scary on the mossy walls. Afterwards we had all dressed up in old-fashioned clothes to have our picture taken. Jake and Dad had put on funny brown waistcoats and hats and Mum smiled down from the photo in a long pale dress, nipped in at the waist, with her hair tied up and wearing a large white hat. She held the small petticoated me in her arms. The lacy dress completely covered my legs. The good thing about that photo is that you can't see that there is anything wrong with me.

The wall behind the spare room door was lined with shelves of photograph albums, all labelled with the year. I eased down the large black album from the year I was born, struggling under its weight. The first few pages showed a family barbeque in our old house. Gloria was there, in a pair of purple boots that came up to her thighs, with four-inch heels. Some things never change. Mum wasn't in the first few pictures because she always liked to be the one holding the camera. She graduated as an art student and had always planned to go into interior design. Last year she had started doing a course, but now, with a new baby on the way...

There was a picture of Dad, before the grey hair, wearing a chef's hat and turning the meat on the barbeque. He was raising a toast to Mum's camera with a large bottle of beer. And here was Jake, covered in mud with tomato ketchup spouting out of the corner of his mouth, looking like a miniature werewolf. Opposite was my favourite picture of Mum. She had a sparkle in her eye and was smoothing down her blouse to show off her pregnant tummy.

I turned the next page of the album slowly, knowing that on the other side were pictures of myself, born only days after the barbeque, a tiny, blue looking creature with tubes and wires all over it. There were the anxious, tired faces of my parents, Jake looking sad and confused. I didn't want to see any more. Shutting the album, I replaced it on the shelf.

My eyes scanned the rows. There was the album from Jake's birth, decorated in angelic babies with wings and halos. *Please, if there's a God, can this pregnancy end like Jake's?*

I decided not to look at the angelic baby album with all its happy faces, pulling out instead the one from my first year at school and leafing through it. I had insisted on standing up for the picture of me in my first school uniform, me in the middle, with Jake and Dad on either side. They were both supporting me, but it looked as though we were about to do a line dance. It had felt so good to be going to school like Jake. Back then I had no worries, no fears, as I faced the big wide world... And there was Jake helping me with my reading at the kitchen table. Oh yes, and Jake pushing the old wheelchair in the egg and spoon race at Sports Day.

I put the album back and took out last year's. We were at the beach at Widemouth. Jake was carrying me into the water, knees bent, staggering under my weight but determined that he should be the first to take me into the sea. You couldn't see our faces because Mum was standing behind us on the beach taking the picture but there was Jake's perfectly formed back in his bright green swimming trunks and my arm behind him, legs and head dangling on either side. How Jake managed it without dropping me I couldn't say, because we were laughing so much.

My tummy rumbled loudly, and I wondered when dinner would be ready. I put the last album back and decided to go to my bedroom and put the telly on for a while.

I had chosen the colours in my room. It was mostly lilac with one pink feature wall behind the bed. There was a warm lilac fleece on the bed and fluffy white scatter cushions. It was a big room with plenty of space for my wheelchair. There was also a large, comfortable armchair, covered in a sheepskin rug. I always looked forward to getting out of the hard wheelchair in the evenings after school and sinking into my armchair to watch TV or play computer games. Easing forward in my chair I lifted the footplates on which my feet rested, then dragged myself out of the wheelchair and flopped onto the sheepskin, flicking on the TV. I curled up my legs and hugged them.

Chapter 9

It was after seven when Dad's headlights flashed across my ceiling as he pulled onto the drive. He must have sat in the car for a while because I went into the hall just in time to see him walking in and Gloria trotting out of the living room looking flustered.

"Anthony! I didn't hear the car. Let me take your coat. Can I get you a beer?"

"Black coffee. I'm going back to see Liz again later."

Gloria scampered off past me. Dad looked down.

"Evening, my Princess," he smiled. But it was a weary smile.

Jake came down the stairs at a run.

"What's going on? Harriet says Mum's in hospital. What happened?"

Dad couldn't look him in the eye.

"We don't really know, son. Mum's OK now, but she had a funny turn this morning. Mrs Turner next door had to call an ambulance."

The Warthog! It should have been Mum phoning an ambulance for her, she's the old one.

"Blooming heck! An ambulance?"

"No need for that kind of language, Jake," said Dad, but his heart wasn't in it. "The doctors think it was a one-off, but they're keeping her in for a few days to be sure. Let's see what Gloria's been cooking shall we? I'm ravenous, I haven't eaten all day."

Dad was a tall man with long cuddly arms. If I was his princess then Dad was certainly my king, big and strong and always so much in control. I felt safe when Dad was at home. He took the back of the wheelchair and pushed the front wheels into the air so that my head fell backwards. Giggling, I looked into his eyes. *I love you*, they said, *everything's gonna be alright*.

Alan was already at the table, sitting in Mum's place, waiting to be served.

"A'right there, mate?" he asked, grinning up at Dad as though he was the Cheshire Cat and this was the Mad-Hatter's tea party instead of a family emergency. "If you're hungry, you're in for a treat. Gloria serves up a wicked beef stew. And I have it on good authority there's apple pie and custard for afters."

After dinner, Gloria fussed round, stacking the dishwasher – even though it was Jake's job.

"Young boy like you, I'm sure you've got better things to do, my love. You just rest and put your feet up. You've been at school all day."

Dad raised his eyes to the ceiling and gave Jake a nod.

"Right then, Princess," Dad said to me. "You go along and start running the bath; I'll be with you in a bit. I need a word with Gloria."

I wanted to listen at the door, but Dad watched me along the corridor and then shut the kitchen door. I yawned. All the worry had made me tense up, but maybe the warm water would help. The hot water tap coughed as I turned it on. I glared at the large metal and plastic seat that hung on a pole next to the bath. It was the hoist that lifted me in. When I was little, Dad would sweep me up high in his arms and hold me hovering over the bath, teasing me with the warm bathwater. I sighed and went to get my towel and nightie from my room. When I got back to the bathroom, Dad was frothing up the bubbles.

"We'll wash your hair with the shower hose," he said perching on the edge of the bath. "Put your stuff on the stool and get undressed."

Mum always took my clothes off for me, which was much quicker, but Dad used bath-time as a lesson in 'self-help skills'. He usually made it fun even though it was tiring. Tonight, he seemed distracted – well, so was I. I managed to get my blazer off and undo my tie.

"You do my buttons."

"You do two and I'll get the rest." He always had to push me.

The buttons took all my concentration. Once I had manoeuvred my way out of my blouse, I used the bath rail to stand up. Holding on with one hand, I struggled with my skirt and tights.

"Can't."

"OK. You are stiff tonight."

He helped me with the rest of my clothes and got me into the hoist. I pressed the button which lifted the white plastic seat up and over the side of the bath. The cold air gave me goosebumps. Dad lowered the hoist which was infuriatingly slow and finally I felt the crisp bubbles on my legs and then the warm water beneath.

Dad washed my hair and I asked the question that had been choking me up inside.

"Is the baby alright?"

"What's that?" asked Dad, drying his hands on his work trousers.

"The baby?" I signed, so that Dad could not mistake what I was asking.

"How long have you known?"

"This morning."

"Mum told you this morning?"

Yes.

"Does Jake know?"

No.

"Ah," Dad turned on the hose to rinse off the shampoo. "Shut your eyes."

"Dad? Is the baby OK?" I asked again when the water had run clean and Dad had turned off the shower tap.

"Oh yes. The baby seems fine. Being pregnant just doesn't seem to agree with your mother."

Dad pressed the button to lift the hoist out of the water.

"Was it my fault?" I asked as water sloshed off my body.

"Sorry, I didn't catch that. Say it again," said Dad, looking at his watch and reaching for the towel.

"Was it my fault?" I repeated, struggling to speak more clearly this time.

"How could it be your fault?"

"Don't know." I didn't. It was just that Mum needed her rest and she had to spend so much time and energy looking after me.

"Of course not, Princess, don't worry. None of this is your fault."

I got into my chair and pulled my nightie on and we went along to my bedroom. As Dad dried my hair I gazed at his rugged face in the mirror, my eyes roaming over every crease, the greying hair, the line of stubble, the vibrant blue eyes with their long dark lashes. He pulled my mousey hair out taut with the brush, running up and down with the hair drier, taking plenty of time to make sure it was completely dry.

"Story?" I asked when Dad had finished drying my hair and was gathering it into bunches to stop it getting knotted overnight.

Although my request was accompanied by the Makaton sign for 'book', Dad never read from a book, instead he made up the best stories himself, using funny voices and sound effects. But he was looking at his watch again.

"No, darling, I have to get back to Mum before visiting time is over."

I didn't push it.

Helping me to my feet, Dad suddenly grabbed me under my arms in a massive bear hug and spun me in a swirling cuddle. I nuzzled into his scratchy face.

"You're too big," he chuckled, laughter lines replacing all the worry wrinkles on his face. He plonked me playfully on the bed. "Shall I put some music on for you?"

I nodded, pulling the covers up under my chin. Dad pressed the switch on the CD player. He kissed my forehead and soul music filtered through the air.

"I'll say 'hi' to Mum for you?"

I nodded.

"Don't worry your little head, Princess. And don't forget to turn out the bedside light. Na-night."

I watched him leave.

Night Mum, I thought. *Come home soon.*

Chapter 10

I woke up late the following morning. It had been a bad night. I thought that Jake would have come downstairs to see me once Dad left, but he never appeared. I heard him talking on the phone in his bedroom until after eleven.

It was odd having Gloria and Alan staying in the house, as though even the house could feel their presence. My ears strained to hear their unfamiliar sounds. In the late darkness, long after my music had finished and Alan and Gloria had gone to their room, I heard Dad come home. His footsteps were heavy and slow on the stairs as he went up to bed.

When I did finally get to sleep, I kept having strange dislocated dreams, from which I woke only to gaze at the dark ceiling above. The dreams became more and more disturbing so that I was reluctant to fall asleep again. But the thoughts in my conscious mind were just as worrying. Eventually, just before dawn, I fell into a heavy black sleep that no longer troubled me. Dad woke me at eight, stroking my hair.

"Breakfast time! Up you get."

I struggled into my wheelchair and went to brush my teeth. It's always my first priority in the morning. It is uncomfortable enough to wake up in this useless body without having to live with that grungy taste. When I got to the kitchen, it seemed that everyone had overslept. I had never seen my grandmother without four inches of make-up. Gloria was wearing a black silk dressing gown with a red rose embroidered on the back and her pyjamas were cotton, with a big flowery pattern so that she almost looked like a normal grandmother – except for the kitten-heeled slippers and the black-painted toenails. Alan didn't appear for breakfast.

"How was Mum last night?" asked Jake.

"Not sure," sighed Dad, reaching over for the jam. "Very tired. I think they'll have to keep her in for a bit."

"Why? What's wrong with her, Dad?"

"They're running tests," Dad hesitated. "She's pregnant, Jake."

"Oh."

There was silence as Dad put toast on my plate. Mum would have buttered it for me, but there was no point asking Dad. I picked up my knife and stabbed holes in the margarine, getting more toast in the spread tub than spread on my toast.

"Dad look what she's done! Do you want a new knife for the marmalade, Harriet?" asked Jake.

"I'll get it for her, dear," said Gloria getting up.

"How pregnant is she?"

"Not sure, son. I don't think she realised." His voice sounded bitter. Perhaps Mum hadn't told him.

The marmalade got all over the table and the toast was a nasty mushy mess. Still, I had done it all by myself. I shut my eyes so that I didn't have to look at it. It tasted OK.

"So, what's wrong? Is this like... before?" Jake asked tentatively.

"A bit," Dad's voice wavered.

I stared at the sticky table and the toast turned to coal in my throat.

"What time does the taxi come?" asked Gloria bringing everyone back to the here and now.

"Twenty minutes! Hurry up with that toast, Princess. I'll pour you some juice." Dad put down his own toast and pushed it aside, wrinkling his nose as though it was crawling with maggots.

Even though there was so little time Dad still tried to make me dress myself, so we were late, and Sam had to wait. I snarled at Alan's Goldwing as Dad took me down the drive. If I was a Rottweiler, I'd puncture its tyres.

"So, where's your Mum, Harry?" Sam asked once we were in the minibus and on our way. "Is she sick?"

I nodded.

"Oh dear, I'm sorry. Is that why you've got the dragon there?"

I smiled half-heartedly. *Yes.*

"Bet she's OK really, is she? The dragon?"

I made a face.

The rest of the journey passed quietly. I watched the streets roll by without really seeing them. I couldn't help thinking that Mum's pregnancy was a bad idea. Dad had said it himself – this was how things had started to go wrong when I was born.

Chapter 11

I felt bad enough when I got to school; but it didn't help when Charlotte said, "My God, Harriet! You look awful. Didn't you sleep very well?"

No.

"You look like you've been crying."

I shook my head. I wished Charlotte wouldn't look at me like that – it made me want to cry again.

"Are you sure you're OK?"

Yes.

"If you say so. We'd better hurry up, we're late for registration."

"Into your places, girls," Mrs Jenkins barked as we entered the classroom. "Harriet, Mrs Alcott won't be in today. You'll just have to muddle along."

Well at least that meant I wouldn't get a repeat of yesterday afternoon, with Mrs Alcott trying to get me to speak every two minutes. Perhaps she'd have forgotten about it by the time she got back.

Charlotte and I had to go round the long way to the Science block to avoid the steps. It was cold outside, and a thin hazy drizzle hovered in the air.

"I wish summer would hurry up," shivered Charlotte almost falling off the path as she tried to walk along next to the wheelchair.

I knew what she meant. I feel the cold more than most people. It makes my muscles contract and my joints seize up, so that they feel and look even more awkward than usual.

The Science block was quite new, but Mr Basing, the Chemistry teacher was ancient. He had mottled grey hair, most of which grew out of his ears so that he looked like a wise old tawny owl. He stood at the front of the class, peering over his half-moon glasses, waiting for silence.

"No Mrs Alcott today?" he asked.

I shook my head.

"Never mind, Harriet. Just let me know if you're having problems."

As if!

The benches in the Science lab were up high, but my group sat at a normal table which had been brought in from another class. As I joined them, Greg and Trescott were arguing in muffled tones about football teams and Tim and Juliette had their books in front of them pretending to be looking over their work from last lesson.

"You OK, Harriet? Have you got everything?" asked Charlotte.

Yes.

Charlotte went off to sit with her friends near the back of the class.

"Right, Class, gather round the middle bench. You don't need your pens with you, but you will all need to be wearing goggles," hooted Mr Basing.

There was a mad rush to the central desk where a tank of water waited.

"Calmly!"

Great, I thought as I turned my chair round. I couldn't see what was happening in Science demos unless Mrs Alcott supported me by balancing me on a stool.

"Harriet, will you be able to see?" asked Mr Basing.

Yes, I lied. I positioned my chair to the side of him, hoping to be able to glimpse the experiment past the row of heads. Greg sat in front of me and kept turning round and making faces when Mr Basing wasn't looking.

The class became quiet. I listened to the edgy anticipation of my classmates and saw the teacher cutting a slice of something with the kind of care James Bond would use to defuse a bomb. Then there was a plop and a hiss. The class simultaneously leant back on their stools.

"Wow!" said Thea.

"Cor blimey!" said Trescott.

There was a sizzle and a splutter, and the tank became silent.

"What was that, Sir?" asked Will.

"Good question, William. Now quietly back to your places everyone."

Greg got down from his stool and deliberately tripped over my wheelchair, making it judder.

"Watch out, Spaz," he sneered.

Spaz! Why do people think it's so original and clever to say that? Of course, I *am* spastic – but only my muscles, not my brain. Greg was just an idiot, a worm under the wheel of my chair.

I went back to the table with the others. My mind drifted as Mr Basing explained the experiment. I looked out of the window. The drizzle had lifted, and moody black clouds were sculling across the sky amid patches of pale blue. The sun was trying to shine. Jake's class was out playing rugby on the field looking cold and muddy, but Jake and Cameron weren't watching the ball; they were sheltering from the wind beside the hedge. The PE teacher blew the whistle and told them off, making them re-join the game.

I jumped when Mr Basing said my name.

"You work with Juliette," he told me.

We had to do some experiments with water and metal and fill in a chart. Nothing much seemed to happen. It was nice working with Juliette though. She respected the fact that I didn't want to talk, and she was quite happy to lead the experiments. And Juliette used pointing and miming herself, because her English was still patchy.

"That was a really good experiment. Could you see it?" Charlotte asked as we went back to the main building after the lesson. The wind wasn't so cold, but it was strong. It picked up my plaits and slapped them against my back.

I shook my head.

"I didn't think so. I'd quite like to watch it again – we could go into the library and see it on that website Mr Basing gave us?"

I was too surprised to say 'no'.

The library was a good place to go at lunchtime to help pass the time, but I had never gone with anyone else outside lesson time. We had to ask for special permission from the librarian, because we weren't supposed to use the library at break, but she was fine about it once Charlotte had explained.

"How nice of you, my dear. Do you need any help?" she whispered. It was one of the things I loved about the library – the peace and quiet.

"No, we're fine."

Once I had seen the demonstration on the internet, I could see why the class had been so impressed. As well as looking up the reaction of sodium with water, we also watched a demonstration of potassium and water. The tank actually exploded!

"Blimey!" I said accidentally.

Charlotte smiled at me. "Yes. Blimey," she repeated softly.

The bell went for second lesson and Charlotte and I went to Geography. Charlotte actually went up to Mr Henderson and asked if she could sit next to me because Mrs Alcott was away! She sat next to me in English after lunch as well. Charlotte was better at explaining things than Mrs Alcott.

Charlotte was in a different class for Maths, so for the last lesson, I was on my own again. I had to put up with Greg and Trescott, and they were much rowdier when Mrs Alcott wasn't there. But I didn't care; Charlotte had made me feel like a real person.

Chapter 12

"Hey, you're looking chirpy, Harry. Good day?" asked Sam as he helped me into the car.

Yes. It had been. I looked out of the window at the daffodils nodding in the pale sunlight.

"So, do you want to hear how I got on with Evette last night?"

Sam had got the chair into the cavernous boot and started up the car.

Ooh Yes! I had forgotten all about Sam's date.

He described his evening, how Evette had asked lots of questions and seemed really interested in his job.

"I got scared though – I didn't make another date. But I do want to see her again – tonight?"

I shook my head.

Sam looked disappointed.

"You don't think she'll want to see me again?"

Yes!

"She will? ...but I shouldn't try to see her tonight?"

That's right.

"So, I phone her up and see if she wants to see me another night?"

Yes! Exactly.

I smiled to myself – how did I get to qualify as relationship councillor? Maybe I just counted as Sam's friend.

The Goldwing still guarded the house when we got back to Apricot Avenue, bringing my spirits crashing to the ground again.

"Looks like the dragon's still here," said Sam as he parked the car next to the motorbike on the drive.

Gloria came out of the house. She was wearing an emerald green top today and had painted her nails to match.

"See you tomorrow," called Sam as he pulled the door shut behind Gloria. In the hall, I tried to signal to Gloria to put the chair onto auto so I could steer myself.

"Yes, yes, dear. I'll take you to watch TV with Alan," said Gloria, not looking at me.

I gave up.

"Hello, girlie," said the gargoyle in Dad's chair. "Jonny Freeman's got trouble with this young geezer! You like watching the darts with me, don't you Hun?"

I smiled in defeat.

Chapter 13

I sat there seething in the semi-dark, the six o'clock news flickering silently on the TV screen. Dad had arrived back from the hospital with Jake about twenty minutes earlier. Jake had stormed up to his bedroom and slammed the door and Dad didn't even say a word! Then Alan got up from his chair without turning up the volume on the TV (which he had put on mute so that he could read his newspaper) and without passing me the remote control. He smiled at me and ruffled my hair and then disappeared off to see Dad in the kitchen. There the adults had gathered like a pack of whispering wolves.

I couldn't believe Dad had taken Jake to see Mum and not me. How was she? Was it so bad that no one wanted me to know?

Alan went to the bottom of the stairs and called, "Dinner time!" and when Jake came down, they started eating – without me!

"Hey! What about me?" I called, but try as I might, my voice was feeble. Nobody heard.

I waited. Furious.

Finally, Dad exclaimed, 'Where's Harriet?!' and I heard him dragging his chair back from the table.

"Where is she going to sit?" Alan asked.

"You didn't even lay her a place? Gloria!"

"Hush, hush. Move along, Jake."

Dad flicked on the sitting room light so that I blinked in the sudden glare.

"Why didn't you come when we called?" Dad asked irritably.

"My chair!" I motioned behind me. Why did Dad have to speak to me like that? It was hardly my fault.

"Right, OK. We'll have to explain to Gloria. Sorry, Harriet."

Gloria was raising the flap of the table and setting another place when Dad and I came into the kitchen. Embarrassment hung in the air like red mist.

"Gloria!" Dad said sharply. "Do you even know how to put this chair onto auto?"

"Err?" She sounded stupid. Dad showed her which button to press on the chair.

I looked straight at Gloria. *That's what I was trying to tell you when I came home!*

"Ah! Now I see," she said awkwardly.

Gloria put a plate of food in front of me and everyone shuffled back into place around the table. I was next to Jake, with Dad opposite and Gloria and Alan on either end. They all pretended to be busy with their food, but I could see them swapping guilty looks. And so they should. Anger burned in my throat and stung my eyes – how dare they? I glowered at the plate of pie and peas feeling nothing in the world would tempt me to eat it. They all deserved to watch me die of starvation before their very eyes.

"So, Anthony, dear, what've you decided about your trip?"

"Well… I have to go."

But Mum isn't here to look after us.

Jake was incredulous. "You're actually going?"

"Your mother's going to be fine. She'll be home in a day or so."

I couldn't believe this was happening.

"But Anthony! I'm not sure I can do it."

"You'll be fine, Gloria. I've never asked before and you know I can't afford to lose this contract… not with this baby on the way"

I looked at Dad, through tear-heavy eyes. He was hunched over his food as though trying to shield off hailstones.

"No!"

"Don't you start, Harriet!" Dad's voice whipped the air and landed like a slap on my face. I was stunned. He never spoke harshly to me, and that was twice in one evening.

"I'm sorry, Gloria. I can't eat this." Dad said at last, his voice quavering. "I'm going to pack."

I watched him leave, then glared round the table – wasn't anyone going to do something about this? Jake threw his cutlery down and rushed out of the room slamming the door behind him. Gloria's mouth flapped open vacantly, eyes staring straight ahead like a fish laid out on ice at the market. But Alan's manner was the most infuriating. He had adopted an air of mild disinterest, as though the whole thing had nothing whatever to do with him and he was wondering if he should start a conversation about the weather.

The bright peas on my plate laughed at me through bubbles of salt water as the tears fell freely down my face.

Mum! What's going on? Please come home.

Chapter 14

I was trapped in the kitchen with Mr and Mrs Gargoyle. The kitchen door was stiff. I knew I couldn't open it myself and I hated asking for help.

"Well," said Alan when he had finally finished his food.

"He can't just bugger off like this," Gloria spluttered.

"Gloria! There's a young-un present."

"Well, babes, we're supposed to be away this weekend and we've already had to cancel the party tomorrow. He shouldn't expect me to drop everything just like that. It's not on."

"A man's gotta do what a man's gotta do. He don't want to go, love, but he's got to. We'll just have to make the best of it."

I lifted my hand to my eyes and tried to dry my face. He couldn't just go, could he? I looked at Gloria. All the natural colour had drained from her face making her look suddenly old. The brown 'heaven's tan' foundation had congealed into the cracks and her blusher made her look like a clown. A tear trickled from the corner of one eye.

"I don't think I can do it, Alan." Gloria's voice was barely audible.

Alan pushed his chair back from the table.

"Come here, love," he said, patting his knee.

"Anthony might come down."

"Love!" said Alan, getting up. He actually gave Gloria a cuddle right there, in front of me. "You're the strongest woman I've ever met. You can handle anything."

Now he was kissing the silly peroxide hair! I looked at the patterns in the dark slate floor. I could hear Dad knocking on Jake's door.

"Let me in, Jake... Jake. I'm leaving now..."

He really was going!

"I'll see you in three weeks, son. Be good for... for Gloria. And for your Mum when she gets back. Jake?"

"Just go, Dad!" Jake yelled. There was an almighty crash. He must have thrown something.

The suitcase went thump, thump, thump on the stairs. Gloria jumped up, pushing Alan away and began to clear the table. Alan's plate was empty, but the other four had barely been touched.

"Waste of good food," she sniffed.

The door opened.

"Right, guys, I'm off. I'll be going straight from the hospital, so I'll see you when I get back."

"OK there, son," Alan slapped Dad on the shoulder. "Don't you worry, mate. We'll hold the fort."

Dad put his suitcase down in the doorway and came over to me, looking like a dog that knows it's been bad. He reached down to hug me.

"Chin up, Princess. Mum'll be home soon."

I refused to hug him back. How *could* he leave like this?

"Just so you know, Harriet. There's no internet access where I'm going. It's the back of beyond."

Good. I don't even want *to be in touch with you.*

"Gloria," said Dad, straightening up at last.

Gloria spread a smile thickly on her face.

"Now, now, dear, don't you worry about a thing. Have you got everything you need? Oh, your keys!"

"Wouldn't get far without these," Dad joked feebly, picking them up from the kitchen worktop.

"Drive carefully, love. And have a good trip," said Gloria, beaming like Christmas lights in July.

He was gone.

Gloria sank back down into her chair and her mask fell off again. She put her hand to her head and knocked Mum's favourite mug off the table with her elbow. It splattered on the floor with a loud, hollow splinter. It was

66

the one that I had painted at primary school. Faded now, it was yellow with little pink and purple dots all over it.

"Oh... fiddledy fuggers!" said Gloria.

"Now, come on, Gloria, clear that up in a minute. I'll put the kettle on, and you can make us both a good strong cuppa tea. You'll be fine."

I decided to leave them to it now the kitchen door was open. I drove the chair carefully round the shards of china and into the hall.

Where are you, Jake?

Jake opened his bedroom door just at that moment, as though he'd heard me thinking. I watched him come down the stairs. His face was like fire and he didn't look at me.

"Ake?" I asked when he reached the bottom of the stairs.

"Get out of my way, Harriet," he snarled, shoving past my chair.

He grabbed his coat and charged out of the house. The hall shuddered as the door banged shut.

Gloria hurried out of the kitchen and followed him out.

"Jakie, dear!" she called.

"I'm going out," he bellowed from the drive.

"No problem, lovey. See you later." Gloria came in and shut the door gently.

"Of course, he'll want to see his friends, won't he?" she said as she walked past me and back into the kitchen.

"Course he will. He'll be back," said Alan.

Great! I thought. *Who am I meant to talk to now?*

In my room, I selected one of my old DVDs, 'Beauty and the Beast'. It was a bit babyish, but it was comfortable.

Which enchantress put a spell on me? I wondered as I clambered into my armchair and kicked off my shoes.

Chapter 15

Gloria tapped lightly on the bedroom door and walked into the room sideways, like a crab, as if she couldn't face what had to be done.

"We'll have to turn the telly off and get you into bed," she said, stepping in front of the screen and turning it off at the switch.

There was only ten minutes left to run on my film. Couldn't she have left it on?

"So, what do we have to do?"

I pointed at the wheelchair.

Gloria seemed to be bracing herself.

"Right," she said. She shuffled up towards me and reached out to put my legs on the floor. Realising Gloria's intention, I struggled upright.

"Err... OK. How do we get you up? I know what I'll have to do."

"Wait!" I said.

But Gloria didn't even realise I had spoken. She took hold of my hands and tried to pull me up. But my feet slid on the floor.

Help!

"This isn't going to work," yelped Gloria.

My legs had slipped right out from underneath me and Gloria was pulling me by the wrists. I was totally at her mercy. Pushing up against me, Gloria managed to manoeuvre my bottom precariously back onto the edge of the armchair.

"I can't do it. I knew I wasn't strong enough to lift you."

You're not supposed to lift me.

"What am I going to do?" Gloria was still using her body to hold me tenuously on the chair. I had become rigid with fright. I was sliding down. What would happen if I fell onto the floor? I'd never get up then. Why hadn't Gloria just waited for me to get myself into the wheelchair?

"Alan, come quickly," Gloria yelled. She shifted her bodyweight and I started slithering down towards the floor. She yanked my arms, trying to hold me. "Hurry! Alan!"

"What the hell...? You'll give me a heart attack," shouted Alan, charging into the room.

He came to a dead stop and gazed at us in disbelief. Me, only inches from the floor, Gloria tugging my arms, trying to pull me back up.

"You'll break her bleedin' arms like that! Let her down onto the floor. Now!"

"Are you sure?"

"Don't worry, I'll get her back up."

Gloria looked relieved and allowed me to slide gently to the floor. She stood back as Alan crouched down next to me.

"Are you OK?" he asked.

I smiled a tense, feeble smile.

"I've got you," said Alan. He eased one arm under my back and the other under my legs and lifted me back into the armchair.

Gloria watched, her arms by her side.

"Thanks," she said. Then she realised. "Oh no – I was trying to get her into the wheelchair."

"No problem. I'll put her in for you," he said bending down again. He smelt of fabric softener and stale tobacco. His cravat tickled my nose.

"Wait!" I said.

"Hang on," said Alan, straightening up. "How did she get out of her wheelchair in the first place?"

"What do you mean?" asked Gloria.

"Well, did you put her in the armchair?" Alan asked with mounting annoyance.

"No. Maybe Jake did."

"Jake's gone out, you silly woman."

They were quiet for a while.

"Did you get out of your chair by yourself?" asked Alan.

I nodded.

"Does that mean you can get back in it yourself?"

Yes! I was so relieved. It was no good anyone trying to help. I was too big now.

Gloria sank down onto my desk.

"It's a shame she can't tell us these things," she sighed.

"Maybe she can – if you just ask her," snapped Alan. "I'll leave you two to it then, shall I?"

Gloria hung her head as he left the room.

"OK. Show me how you do it then, Harriet," she said, shamefaced.

I still felt shaky, but I managed to drag myself into my wheelchair. Gloria was very quiet. She followed me out of my bedroom without a word. I signalled to her to stay outside the bathroom while I went in alone. I couldn't deal with Gloria watching me go to the toilet! When I emerged from the bathroom ten minutes later, Gloria was still waiting where I had left her, wringing her hands like a naughty schoolgirl. She followed me back to the bedroom and got in the way while I looked for a clean nightie in the chest of drawers. I struggled out of my blazer, then motioned to Gloria, *take off my tie and shirt.*

Gloria undid the tie and buttons obediently and I put my nightie over my head. I stood beside the bed and struggled with my tights myself. I wasn't having Gloria help any more than absolutely necessary.

Gloria pulled back the duvet and I climbed into bed. We couldn't look at each other.

"Night, Harriet," Gloria mumbled as she left. "Sleep well."

I stared into the darkness.

That had to have been the worst evening of my life! I was furious with Dad, worried about

Mum and embarrassed and completely exhausted from Gloria. At least with all that emotion I fell asleep straight away.

Chapter 16

I woke up early the following morning. The wind was blowing the shed door outside, a relentless bang... bang... bang. Dad would go mad. But Dad wasn't there. Nor was Mum. There was only Gloria and Alan. I felt a rush of embarrassment and frustration when I thought about Gloria and decided to put her out of my mind. I wondered what time Jake had come home last night. I hadn't heard him. Where had he gone? The only kid from school who lived close by was Andy. He usually walked back from school with Jake and sometimes he would come in on his way home, often with a packet of Haribos for me. Jake and Andy liked to go into the garage and have a jam on Dad's drum kit. But Andy's Mum was strict. He had to do his homework after tea. So, Jake couldn't have gone there.

I had History first lesson. I hadn't done my homework. The clock beside the bed said it was only six-thirty, but I decided to get up anyway – I would only lie there worrying. I clambered into my chair, dragged a blanket around my shoulders and went over to the computer. As it was starting up, I thought of

Andy. He was gorgeous. If he could fall in love with me before my eighteenth birthday, perhaps the enchantress's spell would be broken. I'd become the beautiful dark-haired princess and we'd live happily ever after. I pushed my chair back from the computer and pressed the knob to the right so that it spun on the spot like Beauty in the Ballroom Scene.

The computer beeped into life and sighing I came to a stop in front of the screen. I typed 'Henry V111' into Google. Old Henry had loads of wives, but I was surprised to find that he'd also had lots of children. I copied and pasted the names and fates of the old boy's wives into a Word document, with a list of all his children, which showed that of his eleven kids, eight had died within the first two months, leaving only Mary, Elizabeth and a son called Edward.

Would I have died within the first two months of my life if I had been born in the 1500s? I thought of the photos in the big black album. I didn't think I'd have lasted the night. The thought sent a shiver down my spine.

After printing off my homework and packing my school bag, I decided to check my e-mails. There was a new message from Auntie Wendy in South Africa:

Darling. I hear Mummy's in hospital. It's times like this I wish I lived closer to you all. I'm sure Mum will be out soon, and your Dad is so good

to you. Everything will be fine. Let me know if there's anything I can do, won't you, Harriet? And let me know how Mum is.
Love you lots… big kisses, Wendy.
P.S. Here's a photo of your cousins I've been meaning to send you.

I clicked on the attachment file. Daren and Kirsten were in their swimming pool, waving. Kirsten was only four and she could swim already. I wondered if we'd still be able to go on holiday to Cape Town this year to visit them. Wendy had come to England lots of times, but this was to be my first trip to South Africa. Jake and I were really looking forward to going on a proper family holiday abroad. The tickets were already pinned to the kitchen notice board.

I clicked the reply box and typed out a message:

Auntie Wendy. You won't believe it. Dad had to go away for work. Gloria's looking after us. It's terrible. She dropped me on the floor yesterday and she smashed the mug I made for Mum in year 3. I don't know what to do. Your loving niece, Harriet Mary Harris.

I pressed the send button and prayed that Wendy would get on the next plane to England.

It was now nearly eight o'clock and the wind was still howling outside and lashing rain onto the window. Gloria must be up now. I closed the computer down and went into the hall. Behind the spare room door, I could hear an alarm clock bleeping pathetically, but no other movement. Was Gloria deaf? I went to the bathroom. Brushing my teeth, I caught my reflection in the mirror. I looked a mess but washing my face didn't help much.

Gloria was rushing out of the spare room tying up her dressing-gown when I came out of the bathroom.

"Good. You're up. Where's Jake? Jake!" she called. "Jake, have you seen the time?"

Gloria followed me into the kitchen and started banging around in the cupboards.

"You can have cereal, it's quick and easy. Now where did I see it? These early mornings! I'm starting to feel my age." There was only dust in the Rice Crispies box, so she chucked it away. "You'll have to have Weetabix."

Yuck, I thought as Gloria threw two into a bowl and slopped milk on top. She shoved them on the table under my nose with a spoon and tottered out of the room. Whoever thought of putting heels on slippers? I wondered. I looked at the Weetabix with distaste. I'd have to eat them, I was starving.

"Jake... Jakie... we're late, love. Up you get! No, you have to get up for school, dear."

I had finished my cereal by the time Gloria managed to persuade Jake to come downstairs. He glared at me as he walked into the kitchen.

"OK, Ake?"

"Shut up, Harriet," Jake replied.

It stung for Jake to speak like this. He was generally so easy going – we had always been friends as well as brother and sister.

"What... I done?"

"Just leave me alone."

"Hush there, Jake. Let me get you some cereal. There's only Weetabix," soothed Gloria.

"Don't want none."

"You must have something, dear."

"I'll get my own breakfast."

"OK, love. Don't worry so much. Mum'll be fine, just see if I'm wrong."

Jake grunted.

"Right then, Harriet, come along. Let's get you dressed." Her eyes were shifty. She was embarrassed, you could tell she was dreading helping me get dressed. I was dreading it too and kept my eyes shut as much as possible, wishing I was somewhere else.

Jake had only just left when Sam rang the doorbell. He was going to be late for school.

"Oh, my goodness, look at the state of me – I can't believe I've got to open the door without my make-up. That's something you should never, ever do..." said Gloria as she hurried out of my bedroom.

"I'm sorry young man. We're not quite ready. I've just got to do her hair. You'll have to wait a minute. Sorry, one minute, OK?"

She obviously didn't wait for a reply because she was already back in my room.

"That busy-body, Mrs Watsit next-door! Curtains always twitching."

At least we agree on the Warthog, I grinned wryly.

"And my hair! I must get up earlier tomorrow..."

Chapter 17

The rest of the class was already spilling out of the form room when Charlotte and I got there.

"Sorry, Miss Jenkins, Harriet was late," said Charlotte, batting her eyelashes at the teacher. She always looked as if she was wearing mascara, but she never got told off.

"Two days in a row, Harriet! What's going on? You seem to be getting later and later."

I shrugged and rubbed a trickle of rain from my face. I had got soaked just getting out of the minibus.

"It all seems to be getting too much for you, Harriet. Off you go to your lesson, both of you. There's no need to be late for that as well."

I was disappointed to find Mrs Alcott sitting in her normal place at the dunce's table when we got to the History room.

"Ah, you *are* here," said Mrs Alcott as I parked my chair in the space next to her at the table. "Sorry about yesterday, my son fell off the garden wall and broke his arm. We were ages at the hospital... Did you get on all right – do you need me to go over anything with you?"

No.

"Speak, Harriet."

"No." Bother, she had remembered about making me talk.

"OK, class, settle down," called Mr Plumber, the History teacher, striding into the room wearing a crown and a big black beard. "My name is Mr Henry Tudor and I am your King." His enormous stomach was already the right shape. "I need some wives. Come here Codey, you can be wife number one. Let's find you a nice headdress. How about this velvet one?" he said, dragging a length of purple cloth from the prop box next to his desk. "Who can tell me her name?"

It was just like Mr Plumber. He was into amateur dramatics and enjoyed nothing more than to get everyone up, acting out their History lessons. He made me go to the front of the class and be Henry's fifth wife, Catherine Howard. That meant I had to be beheaded. Mr Plumber got Will to come and chop my head off. Then Mr Plumber dropped my grey silk veil over my face so that no one could see my head anymore and said, "Good riddance!" Everyone laughed.

"That was so funny – Mr Plumber's a nutter," said Charlotte as we went along the upstairs corridor to the lift to go back to the form room for break.

Yes, it was, I grinned.

Charlotte came to an abrupt halt, putting a hand on my shoulder so that I stopped too.

"Don't look now, but it's Tristan in Year 9. He's drop-dead gorgeous."

A Year 9 class was waiting to get into French One, which was obviously their form room.

Which one? I looked at Charlotte inquisitively.

"Blond hair, curls on top," Charlotte whispered. "Pretend he's not there; don't say a word." She giggled. "Well, that was a silly thing to say – I can trust you not to say anything, can't I?"

I smiled and we started moving again. I didn't normally look at boys' faces, at least, not straight away. You could tell a lot by the way they wore their shirt (which didn't mean craning my neck up and looking as though I was staring). If everything was neatly tucked into their trousers – or even worse, their blazer was buttoned up – I didn't even bother. Then there were the guys who wore their shirts on the outside as a status symbol. 'I'm so cool.' That's what that meant. I was interested in the lads whose shirts were partially untucked. For some it was unconscious – either they didn't care what they looked like, or they were the prim and proper ones who'd got caught out. But for some it was pure rebellion. They were deliberately trying to be different from the 'cool dudes' and the 'prims'. These were the ones I liked. The walk was another clue. The prims shuffled along apologetically; the dudes pranced; but the rebels – their step was more purposeful, less self-conscious. They almost stalked.

Tristan looked like a rebel – though I had to admit, he was very good looking for a rebel. But he didn't look as though he cared about his looks. He wasn't doing any of the dude 'hey look at me' things I disliked so much. All that posing about got on my nerves.

"It's a shame all our lessons can't be as cool as Mr Plumber's History classes," said Charlotte, though her mind was obviously still on Tristan.

Then disaster struck. My wheelchair gave a splutter and stopped. I watched Charlotte, still walking along the corridor, still talking, and still not realising that I had been left behind. I banged the arms of the chair in frustration.

Keep moving...

Tristan and his group were loitering outside their class. Two or three of them nudged one another as Charlotte reached them. They looked at her in wonder.

"Hey, Charlotte, isn't it?" Tristan asked.

Charlotte stopped.

"Who me?"

"You talking to yourself?"

His mates all laughed.

Charlotte turned round, very red in the face. I couldn't believe it. Charlotte was going to be so upset with me because the Year 9s had laughed at her, and all because of my stupid chair.

"What happened?" stammered Charlotte as she approached.

I don't know. I pushed the black knob backwards and forwards to demonstrate that the chair wasn't moving. This had never happened before.

Charlotte bent over, trying the knob herself.

"I don't believe it. He knew my name!" she hissed. "How could he have known my name?"

I looked over Charlotte's shoulder. Tristan was strolling towards us. He was definitely a rebel.

"Ssssh," I warned.

Charlotte looked at me and followed my eyes. There was no doubt. He was coming straight towards us. Charlotte straightened up.

"What's wrong?"

"Err... we're not sure... Harriet's chair just stopped."

Tristan walked round the chair. Charlotte had good taste.

"What's the red flashing light?" he asked.

The battery! No one had charged the battery last night.

"Harriet?" asked Charlotte.

"Battery," I said as carefully as possible.

"The battery!" said Charlotte.

"Is there back-up?" asked Tristan.

No.

Tristan was examining the back of the chair.

"You'll have to put it into manual then, I think... try this..."

"Err... OK," said Charlotte. "Ready, Harriet?"

I nodded.

"We might as well go straight to English," said Charlotte, turning the chair around. We needed to be at the other end of the building. "Erm thanks... Tristan."

Tristan hesitated. It was his turn to go red.

"OK, see you round," he said.

.

Chapter 18

To my relief, Charlotte slowed down a bit when we turned the corner and Tristan could no longer see us. I wasn't used to being pushed and felt I had lost control.

"He's as cute as he looks," gushed Charlotte.

I nodded.

"I hope you didn't mind going straight to English? I couldn't face walking past the French room with everyone watching us."

I looked back at Charlotte and gave her a smile to say it was fine. I was just glad she wasn't angry with me.

"At least I know you won't say anything to Codey and the others. They don't know I like someone in Year 9. But the boys in our year are so babyish... Will's OK, but he's too full of himself..."

The English room was Jake's form room. The bell hadn't gone for second lesson yet, so most of the class was still in there, huddled in clusters, chatting. Set aside from the rest of the class, Jake was perched on a desk, deep in conversation with Cameron, who was leaning on another table, his hands in his pockets. Cameron was quite a lot taller than Jake.

"English'll be boring as usual," Charlotte was saying. "Mrs White's so lame..."

Jake was trying to explain something to Cameron. He emptied out his pockets. They were arguing about the two-pound coin in Jake's hand. Eventually Jake gave it to Cameron. That was his lunch money.

The bell sounded and Jake's class started to troop out of the English room and spill onto the corridor. Charlotte moved the chair back a little to allow them to get out. As Jake passed, I put my hand out to touch his arm. He jerked away and grunted, not even looking at me.

"Was that your brother?" Charlotte asked as she pushed me into the empty classroom.

I nodded.

"What's up with him?"

Don't know, I shrugged.

"This is your table, isn't it? I'll get the chair out of the way."

Charlotte moved the spare chair away and pushed me up to the table.

"I still can't believe he actually knows my name," said Charlotte with a distant look in her eyes. She plopped herself in the seat next to me. "He couldn't possibly fancy me, could he?"

I made a face and nodded my head slowly up and down. *Maybe.*

"Hello, girls. You're keen for your English class!" said Mrs Alcott as she walked into the room.

"Kind of," said Charlotte, winking at me. "The battery ran out on Harriet's chair."

"Oh dear, does that mean you have to push her?"

Charlotte nodded.

"Lunchtime'll be a problem," mused Mrs Alcott. "Shall I get one of the other girls to do it?"

"No. That's fine. I'm sure we can manage."

Thanks, I smiled at Charlotte.

I found it very odd having to be pushed around everywhere. It was horrible having to give up the little independence I had, but at least it meant I had someone to spend lunchtime with. Well Codey, Thea and Alice were there too, but they didn't really try to include me in the conversation (mostly about fashion, which I didn't have much to say about anyway – tight jeans and miniskirts were not exactly my thing). Charlotte tried, but it wasn't very easy:

"Do you like that new band, The Monkey Jacks, Harriet?" she asked as we queued up for lunch. "The lead singer is so fit!"

Although I hadn't even heard of them, I pretended to like them anyway.

Year 7 was last on the lunch rota on Wednesdays and there was nothing left except chilli-con-carne which always looked grey and tasted dusty. We found a table near the door. By nature, I'm a messy eater and I usually found a spot on my own at lunch, so I was feeling self-conscious. But the others spent most of the meal giggling and whispering – I reckoned they were talking about boys. I was about to put the last forkful of chilli in my mouth, concentrating on balancing the rice, when someone came up behind me and pulled the chair away from the table.

"Fancy a spin?" jeered Greg.

My fork clattered to the floor, spilling sauce onto my clean white blouse. People on the nearby tables looked round. Charlotte leapt up from her place.

"Leave her alone, Greg!" she yelled.

But Greg wasn't deterred.

"You don't mind coming for a spin with me, do you, Harriet?"

"Gregory Peterson, what is going on?" hollered Mrs Thacker, the short stocky lunchtime supervisor, bustling out from the kitchen, her jowls quivering like a boxer dog with a flea in its ear.

Now everyone in the hall was looking. I felt my face burning up.

"'S'alright Miss. I said I'd take Harriet for a little walk. Her battery's packed up, see?"

"Harriet, do you want Greg to take you off?"

I shook my head.

"No, Miss, I'm looking after her," said Charlotte.

"Put her right back in her place and go and sit outside Mr Elliot's office, Master Peterson. Not a week goes by when I don't have to send you to the headmaster, boy. What's the matter with you?"

I hunched my back and looked at my knees, trying to hide from all the faces. It was Greg who should be squirming, but I knew he was proud of his display and was sauntering off to see Mr Elliot with an enormous grin on his face.

For the rest of lunch, I was worried that I would be sent to Mr Elliot's office to give my side of the story, but fortunately that didn't happen. Greg arrived in the classroom after dinner as cocky as ever. Trescott gave him an encouraging slap on the back. I glared at him. Couldn't he be beheaded like Catherine Howard? He had the same enormous nose and ugly face I had seen on the internet that morning. I imagined myself as Henry's youngest daughter, the nine-year-old Elizabeth, watching the execution of her hated stepmother, her small hand in her father's. Catherine (A.K.A. Greg), wearing Mr Plumber's scrap of grey silk, as the axe fell...

Chapter 19

The last bell of the day sounded in the corridor.

"Are you ready, Harriet?" asked Charlotte at my shoulder. She usually took me to the main corridor and then rushed off to catch her bus.

I looked at Mrs Alcott who was gathering up her things, and signed, *toilet*. There was no way I could wait till I got home. Mrs Alcott wasn't watching. I had to touch her arm and sign again. Charlotte was shifting from foot to foot.

"She needs the toilet, Charlotte," said Mrs Alcott.

"My bus leaves at five past. The driver won't wait."

"That's OK. You'd better head off and catch your bus. See you tomorrow."

"Ok, bye, Mrs Alcott. Bye, Harriet, see you tomorrow." She swung her hair and linking arms with Thea who lived in the same village, she was gone.

"Alice, you walk home don't you?" said Mrs Alcott, raising her voice.

I looked round. Alice and Codey were giggling on the table behind. Will and Michael were talking to them in low voices.

"Alice," repeated Mrs Alcott, a little more sharply.

Alice looked up.

"Yes, Miss?"

"You walk home, don't you? You're not rushing off for a bus?"

"That's right, Miss."

"Can you take Harriet to the toilet and out to the car park and wait with her until her taxi comes please?"

"Suppose so."

Alice dragged her chair out and I heard her slam it back under the table.

"You gonna walk with us, Will?" asked Codey.

"Well… I've got to get back for the dentist tonight…"

"Alice," said Mrs Alcott as Alice took hold of the back of the chair. "She needs someone to wait with her today. You'll need to tell the taxi driver that her battery is flat."

Alice tutted.

"Alice?"

"Al'right, Miss."

"What a pain," said Alice, pushing me out of the art room and turning right, towards the toilets by the main entrance.

"Where are you going, Alice?" asked Codey. "We'll have to take her to the disabled loo."

"What back up by the form room?" groaned Alice.

"Girls, I'm gonna get going. Coming Michael?" said Will.

"Yeah, mate."

"OK, see you guys tomorrow, bright and early," Alice oozed.

"Damn," she said when they were out of earshot. She turned the chair around. "This is such a hassle."

"He's so totally…," began Codey in a dreamy voice.

"I get first pickings. It's a shame Michael's so boring."

"Have you noticed that Charlotte changes the subject now when we talk about Will?" asked Codey, holding the toilet door open while Alice pushed me in.

"I think she's gone off him," said Alice.

The door closed behind me. I sighed. Why was I so upset? I shouldn't be surprised at being ignored. This was how it had been since I started secondary school. Charlotte was the only one who had bothered to say two words to me.

Alice is right, I thought as I washed my hands. I am just a hassle.

Codey pushed me out to the taxi.

"This wheelchair's heavy," she complained.

"Oh, look at him!" said Codey as we went out to the car park and Sam waved at me. "He must be our taxi driver."

"He looks kinda cute," replied Alice in an undertone.

"What happened?" called Sam as they approached.

"The battery's flat, apparently," said Alice, all coy. "We offered to bring Harriet out."

"That was nice of you."

"It was nothing, really."

"Thanks, I'll take her from here. I'll make sure her grandmother knows about the battery. All right, Harriet?"

*

The Warthog was on her side of the drive when the car pulled into 32 Apricot Avenue. She was pretending to be gardening in the weak sunshine but really it was an ambush.

"Hello there, Harriet. How are you getting on?" she said, abandoning her clematis and opening my door. She bent down and her beady eyes bored into me.

I smiled at her, all sweetness. *The day is not improved by having you in my face*, I thought.

"You look so nice with those plaits, dear. Your grandmother's looking after you I see. In my day, you'd have had ribbons of course. Yellow would suit you. I'll have a little look for you next time I'm in town. Your birthday must be coming up soon."

Does yellow suit anyone?

Gloria and Sam were chatting outside the front door. It didn't look as though they were going to rescue me.

"I hope you are keeping up with your work even though your sweet mother isn't here to look after you. I keep telling her that she should get you knitting. My neighbour when I was a little girl was handicapped like you and she did the most useful things. Blankets for my dolls and scarves at Christmas... I hear your mother won't be home for quite a while. Had another funny turn in the hospital they say... Oh dear, you've made a mess on your blouse, you silly girl. Do you think your Grandmother's got nothing better to do with her time than your washing? You should be more careful..."

The Warthog brandished her gardening knife at my chest like a dagger.

"OK, Mrs Turner, how are you? Are you ready, Harriet?" asked Sam.

She waddled backwards, her sharp little eyes glinting at me. Sam helped me back into my wheelchair and waved goodbye, climbing into the car.

"See you tomorrow, everyone – and don't make the same mistake with that battery," he said, his eyes twinkling.

Gloria pushed me into the house and shut the door firmly in Mrs Turner's face. I craned my neck round to watch and grinned at Gloria.

"She's unreal," said Gloria. "It looked like you were getting a right mouthful from her!"

The house seemed unusually quiet.

"OK, Harriet, so we have to charge your battery. You'll have to show me what to do."

I pointed towards my bedroom.

Alan appeared to be out. The TV murmured in the living room. The applause and roars of laughter suggested a chat show.

I showed Gloria how to re-charge the battery.

"I'm sorry about this. You should have told me last night." She sounded awkward at the mention of last night.

I know. I forgot.

"Never mind, Sam says you had two little friends to push you about."

Gloria went out and I checked my e-mails. Nothing. I put the telly on and plonked myself into my armchair.

The evening was long and quiet. I heard Gloria on the phone several times, but otherwise the house seemed silent and empty.

At seven, Gloria came in with half a pizza and a glass of lemonade on a tray.

"Nice little treat, dinner in your room."

I supposed so, but a much better treat would have been beans on toast in the kitchen with Mum, Dad and Jake.

Gloria put me to bed early. The quiet of the house was almost deafening. Jake came home after nine and went straight to his room. I listened as Gloria tried in vain to persuade him to eat.

Chapter 20

Gloria was singing in the kitchen when I got up next morning. She was wearing a red leather mini-skirt and a black sweater that exhibited her cleavage.

It's obscene to be so brown in March, I thought.

"Hello, Harriet. Porridge OK?"

I nodded.

Gloria scooped the saucepan off the stove. The creamy grey liquid puffed and gurgled like a restless volcano. Gloria slopped it into a waiting bowl.

"Morning all," said Jake at the door. "I'm up for porridge."

"Ah, good, dear. You sit yourself down. Would you like brown sugar or maple syrup?"

Jake seemed in better spirits over breakfast, but his eyes were watchful. He kept glancing nervously over my shoulder at a spot near the kettle. I couldn't imagine what was attracting his attention.

"Right then, my dears, let's see if we can't be on time this morning. It's time to get dressed."

Jake scraped his bowl clean and shot upstairs to get ready.

As I left with Gloria, I glanced at the kettle. The only thing that was different from normal was that Gloria's lime-green purse lay on the counter.

Gloria was very chatty this morning which took my mind off the fact that she was helping me with things that only Mum and Dad had ever helped with before. She rambled on about her plans for the day. She was going shopping and she was going to make her special bacon-wrapped chicken for tea, and she wanted to try out a new recipe for chocolate roulade that she had found in 'Bella'. Which vegetables did I like? She was getting the hang of asking questions that I could nod or shake my head to.

Jake hollered 'good-bye' from the hall at eight thirty. It looked as if we'd both be on time for school today.

My hair still needed doing, but there was plenty of time before Sam arrived. The phone rang and Gloria tottered off into the kitchen. It was Cynthia Darling, finalising arrangements for their shopping trip. Time was ticking by. I picked up my schoolbag and my hairbrush and followed Gloria into the kitchen, but it still took a while for Gloria to get the hint.

"Goodness me, Cynthia, look at the time! I'll have to run, I don't want Harriet to be late

99

again or I'll miss my bus, dear. See you at half-nine."

The phone rang again as soon as Gloria returned it to its cradle.

"Hello, Liz, are you OK, love?... Yes, we're nearly ready... My friend called... No, she didn't tell me..." She gave me a meaningful look. "Yes, I can... Do you want to speak to her?"

I took the phone.

"Mum?"

"Harriet, my darling, how are you?" Mum sounded so far away.

"OK. You?"

"They haven't worked out what's wrong yet, but I'll be fine. Don't worry, they say that if everything's stable over the weekend I'll be able to come home on Monday or Tuesday."

Gloria was tugging at a particularly persistent knot in my hair. I winced and drew air sharply through my teeth.

"I'm sorry, dear, I'm trying to be gentle," whispered Gloria.

"What's wrong?" asked Mum.

"My hair."

"Your what?"

"Hair." It was tedious having to repeat myself all the time.

"Ah, your hair? Is Gloria putting your hair up?"

"Mmm."

"How are you getting on with Gloria?"

"...Fine."

"Good. How's Jake? I take it he's already left for school?"

"He's O.K." Was he? I didn't want to worry her, and I couldn't explain how moody he was.

"I'd better let you go. You're going to be late."

"Bye."

"Love you... Harriet...?"

Gloria twisted the last bobble into place. The tiny hairs in the back of my neck were stretched painfully.

"Yes, Mum?"

"Missing you."

I put the phone down. It was difficult to speak on the phone. Draining.

The doorbell chimed its tinny Vivaldi rendition, a pass-me-down from the previous owners of 32 Apricot Avenue, which everyone hated. The tune lodged malevolently inside its small box like a raucous genie that Dad kept promising to evict, but never had the time.

"Ah, Sam!" said Gloria, opening the door with a flourish. "You see, my dear, we're all ready – I just need to fetch Harriet's swimming costume."

So that's why Mum phoned. I wished she hadn't bothered. I hated swimming at school.

"So, where does Mummy keep the swimming things, dear?"

I shrugged. I had no idea – they just appeared by the front door every Thursday morning.

It took Gloria ages to find the costume. Sam was getting fidgety and kept looking at his watch.

"Are we ready?" he asked when Gloria finally emerged triumphant from upstairs, costume and towel in hand. I didn't tell her it was my old one.

"Just about. Liz wanted me to put in the swimming money. My purse is just in the kitchen…"

"Please be quick, my next client gets really annoyed if I'm late. He waits out on the street, you see." Sam really did look worried.

"Well, that's funny," said Gloria coming out of the kitchen looking confused. "I'm sure I had twenty pounds in my purse. I'll have to write a cheque."

Sam was fiddling anxiously with his keys.

"I'll get Harry in the bus," he said.

Gloria emerged from the house, waving the cheque in one hand and a Millets bag in the other.

"For your wet cossie, dear. Now, enjoy your swim and I'll see you later. Toodle-ooo!" she waved.

"I wish this van would go faster," grumbled Sam as we pulled out of the drive. "Mr Simpson is such a cantankerous old codger. I was late yesterday, and he just kept going on about his army days. I got a right telling off."

Chapter 21

When I arrived at school, there was no sign of Charlotte in reception. I waited until the bell sounded and then made my way down to class. Maybe Charlotte's bus was late. The classroom door was shut so I had to knock on it. Most of the doors in the main building were fire doors and far too heavy for me to move by myself. Miss Jenkins opened it.

"We're doing the register, come in quickly."

I felt the eyes of the class on me as I went to my desk.

"OK, Harriet," said Miss Jenkins when she had finished taking the register. "Charlotte doesn't seem to be here today. Do we have any volunteers for Harriet Duty?"

Greg's hand shot up.

"I don't think so, Gregory, after yesterday's little fiasco in the dinner hall," snapped Miss Jenkins, to my relief.

Greg put on his innocent little pixie-boy look.

"Yes, my boy, I do know. It might be a big place, Milton Comprehensive, but word gets around." She almost seemed to be praising him.

"I will do it, Miss," offered Juliette.

"Thank you, Juliette. OK, Class, enjoy your swim," said Miss Jenkins, gathering her things together.

*

The noise of the pool hummed around, the instructors' directions echoing across the pool. I sat at the edge of the water, my feet dangling in. I still wasn't used to all the other Year 7's being able to see how skinny and twisted and pale and wretched my arms and legs were. And my chest was as flat as an eight-year-old's. Lots of the other girls had little buds already beginning to grow. Alice was already a B cup, as she kept boasting in the changing-rooms.

"OK Harriet, let's get you in."

Mrs Alcott and one of the swimming coaches scooped me up, one on each side, and lowered me into the water. It was freezing. When my feet touched the bottom, the water came up well past my waist, supporting my weight so that I could stand. It was a great feeling. Once I was in the pool, I felt almost normal – I could stand up unassisted and even walk, if I held onto my floats. And the diffractions of the water made everybody's legs look deformed.

There were only five other students in the shallow end, and they were all from different form groups, except for Tim. Tim was even more like a hippopotamus in the water than out. When he swam, his whole body was submerged underwater, with just his eyes and nostrils skimming the surface.

I had to get out of the pool ten minutes before everyone else because it took so long to change. I began to dread the getting out even before time. It was so awkward. I had to be hoisted out of the pool by a big metal trolley. The eyes of all the kids queuing on the edge of the pool waiting to swim would be trained on me and the monstrous hoist, idly watching me being dragged from the water like a half-drowned rat.

As I was being hooked up, I saw Neil and Mathew, from Mrs Henderson's class, duck under the water and pull Tim's legs from under him, sending him sprawling underwater. He emerged coughing and spluttering, but he didn't complain to a teacher.

*

During afternoon registration, the door opened, and Mr Elliot came into the form room with Charlotte. The class stood up.

"Good afternoon, Mr Elliot," they sang.

"Good afternoon, 7G. Sit down," said the headmaster. Taking Miss Jenkins to one side, he stood with his back to the class so that he could speak to her privately. He always wore a full suit and whenever he stood still, he clasped his hands behind his back as though they had a mind of their own and had to be kept under control.

Charlotte went to her place. She looked awful. Her eyes were red, and her pale face was splodged and purple. Her hair was combed back into its usual pigtail, but the front looked as though she had travelled through a blizzard and instead of hanging obediently to one side as it usually did, her long fringe was damp and tangled.

"Yes, Mr Elliot. Thank you for letting me know. I'll keep an eye on her," said Miss Jenkins as she held the door open for the head teacher. "Off you go, Class. Juliette, you take Harriet to your next lesson. I need a word with Charlotte."

The class trooped out. Charlotte seemed reluctant to be left behind by her friends. Her big eyes looked scared and lost.

Chapter 22

The Music teacher was like an overgrown swan. His neck was so long that he had to bend to enter the room. He came in and opened his arms wide with a flourish as though conducting an orchestra or stretching his wings. The class hushed immediately.

"Good afternoon," he began.

"Good afternoon, Mr Jones," the class chorused.

"Copy me," Mr Jones called, and clapped out a rhythm, his white shirt-sleeves billowing.

I listened carefully and clapped along with the class.

Charlotte slipped into the room looking just as bad, but now irritated as well.

"Hello, Charlotte, come in and take your place. We're just doing a little exercise to get everyone in the mood. Copy me again, Class. Listen," said Mr Jones.

Everyone echoed the rhythm.

"A harder one!"

The phrase became a little muffled towards the end.

"Put the two phrases together," said Mr Jones, with a twinkle in his eye.

By the end of the lengthened phrase about half the class had given up. But I was following the rhythm easily.

"Let's practise that again!"

After two or three attempts, most of the class were able to follow the extended rhythm.

"OK, here's another phrase," said Mr Jones pulling a sheet of paper close to him. The new rhythm was rather complicated. The class laughed nervously. Only me and two boys were able to follow it to the end.

"Well done, you three! Can any of you repeat the whole thing back to me?" He tapped out all three phrases, one after another, following it on his score sheet. "You go first, Harriet."

I repeated back the whole phrase without any trouble.

"Excellent, Harriet! Phil?"

Phil and Steven both got muddled in the middle.

"Does anyone else want to try?"

No one moved.

"Well, Harriet! Top marks to you! A round of applause please."

I glowed. I knew I was good at remembering rhythms, but I had never realised that other people didn't find it as easy as I did.

"*Tres bien*, Harriet! That was terrific," whispered Juliette under her breath.

"Take out your theory books everyone and give me your homework as I go round the class," said Mr Jones, handing out some worksheets. He was so graceful, swimming round his pond, inspecting the little brown ducks that had drifted into his waters. He came over to me and took my homework which lay on the table.

"That was really good, Harriet. That was a Grade 8 phrase! Singing may not be your forte, but you certainly have an aptitude for music."

It was high praise indeed. He patted me on the shoulder and paddled off. Greg shot me a contemptuous look. I ignored him, but realised that Mrs Alcott was gazing at me, her eyes all shiny.

"We'll have to put a note in your home-school diary, won't we, so that your Mum knows about this? Make sure you show it to her.... Actually, while you get on with Mr Jones's worksheet, I'll go to the office and give her a quick call. I need to catch up with her about some other things."

I grabbed the sleeve of Mrs Alcott's staid, no-nonsense black blouse.

"It's OK, Harriet, don't look so worried. It's good news, I'm sure she'll be really pleased to hear it."

I gave up. It was too complicated to explain. I looked at the worksheet but couldn't focus on it. Would Mrs Alcott find Gloria at home? Probably. It was nearly three o'clock and Gloria had probably started on her chocolate roulade.

"OK Class, I need to fetch something from Music Two. You're in secondary school now, people – you don't need babysitting. I expect silence. Get on with your work."

"He just wants to see Miss Turner – he hasn't seen her for half an hour!" commented Will to the class when Mr Jones had glided out of the room.

"Yer," said Michael. "We all know he fancies her!"

"You mean he's not gay?" leered Trescott, twiddling his pencil between his fingers.

The class tittered and began murmuring to one another.

I didn't really want Mrs Alcott to know what was going on at home. She would start asking questions and trying to make me talk. Greg kicked my chair.

"Chair working again is it? Shame."

I glared at him.

"It's a pity you didn't wanna come for a walk with me yesterday."

I wished I could turn him into stone with one look and a shake of my snake-hair.

"I could have taken you to the top of a cliff and put you out of your misery."

I narrowed my eyes at him. He was the snake.

"Let me see – how do we put it on manual?" Greg asked, reaching round to the back of the chair. "This must be the button here..."

Get lost.

"Let's see if I can bust it..."

"Get away from me! Don't touch my chair!" I yelled.

The whole class fell silent.

"Blooming heck! Was that Harriet?!" asked Will from the other side of the room.

"That was an alien tongue if ever I heard one," Trescott laughed.

"No wonder she doesn't normally talk with a voice like that," said Greg. "Do you come from the planet Zyborg?!" he asked in a loud hysterical voice.

Everyone laughed.

"And what did she actually say?" Will sniggered.

"God knows," said Greg.

Charlotte stood up, knocking her chair onto the floor. Her face was bright red and crunched up with rage.

"Shut up! Shut up the lot of you. I can't stand it. How dare you all laugh? That's the problem in this class nobody cares about anyone else's feelings. Greg you're a... you're a..." Charlotte's mouth opened and shut as though her lower jaw wasn't quite working properly. She was speechless.

"You hear that Greg?" said Trescott in mock disbelief. "You're a..."

"And you three are no better," Charlotte snapped glaring at her friends who were trying to hide their laughter behind their hands. "I'm getting Mr Jones."

"Ooooh!" said Greg. "I'm scared!"

The class giggled.

Charlotte stormed out of the room slamming the door behind her.

"You're in trouble now, Greg," said Alice wiping the laughter tears from her eyes and trying to compose herself.

"Who cares?" said Greg, sticking his chin out. He looked at me and hissed in a breathy voice, "Speak to me..."

A few people snorted.

"I think she'd rather not," gabbled Trescott in a crude mockery of my voice.

Juliette stood up, her face ashen.

"Come, Harriet. You come out with me," she said.

I was relieved and looked at no one as we left the room together. Outside the classroom door, Juliette bent down to me and gave me a hug.

"I am so sorry," she breathed in my ear. "That was horrible. Greg – he is a pig!"

The corner of my mouth twitched in a half smile at the thought of a pig with Greg's head, but tears ran down my face and dripped into Juliette's hair.

Mr Jones marched round the corner of the corridor with Charlotte running beside him to keep up. Mrs Alcott followed at a trot.

"Harriet! Are you all right?" asked Charlotte.

Mr Jones strode past and wrenched open the classroom door.

"What is going on in here?" he bellowed. "What do you lot think...?"

The rest of the afternoon followed in a blur: the sympathetic murmurs from Charlotte and Juliette; the angry disappointment from Mrs Alcott and Mr Jones; the silence and then the chorused apology from the rest of the class as I re-entered the Music room. And later, the 'quiet word' from Mrs Alcott about not telling her Mum was in hospital.

"I think I'd better write a note to your grandma to tell her what has happened in class today," she said.

No.

"Harriet, it's important she knows..."

I shook my head vehemently. What good would it do Gloria knowing how I'd been ridiculed?

"OK, but I didn't manage to get through to your Mum at the hospital earlier. I'll tell her when I call her later on."

No.

"Maybe you're right. She probably has enough on her plate. But I do think you should talk to your grandmother."

Chapter 23

"Are you OK, Harriet?" asked Sam as he helped me into the car. "You look like you've seen a ghost."

I nodded vaguely and gazed into the distance. Greg was walking out of the school gates with Trescott, in an animated mood. Trescott thumped him on the shoulder and said something with a stupid look on his face and his eyes crossed. They both doubled up laughing.

"Evette and I had a brilliant evening last night," said Sam as he clicked his seatbelt in and started up the car. "We went for a walk along by the river and out to the Farmer's Arms."

I mustered all my strength to smile at him, *that's great!*

"I wish you could see her, Harry, she's gorgeous. Her skin is like honey and her eyes are such a deep, honest brown..." he rambled on. At least someone's life was going well.

The town flickered past behind my reflection. I had the odd feeling that my life was happening to someone else. I was being carried along in some other person's useless body and really, I was someone quite different. That old song – 'A mirror never shows the real me.'

Sam pulled up beside the house. Gloria was in the garage and came out wiping spiders-webs from her manicured hands. She was wearing a set of grey joggers, looking like any normal grandmother.

"Hi, Harriet," she called. "Ah, good, you remembered your swimming kit. Sam, Harriet's had a super day today. Her support worker, Mrs Alcott – lovely woman – phoned up... Did you know that Harriet is a musical genius?"

"Well, no I didn't, Gloria. But we do like the FTC Jazz Channel on the radio, don't we, Harriet?"

I nodded and Sam helped me out of the car.

"Jazz! Now isn't that funny? Jazz was always my thing too." It was the first real smile Gloria had ever given me. Well, she'd never had the opportunity to get gooey over my first step or the funny things I said.

"Now, I've had a brainwave! I remembered Anthony's old drum kit in the garage from when he fancied himself as a rock drummer. He was in a real band, you know, in his twenties. What was it they called themselves now? The Madmen of Milton, something like that."

"Was he really?" said Sam. "He has that rocker look about him."

116

"Oh, he was a right looker in those days, Sam." Gloria's face lit up like a bright moon on a dark night. "Do you think you could give me a hand to drag all these bits onto the drive so we can give them a bit of a clean? Or are you in a hurry?"

"No, that's OK, Gloria, I'm done for the day."

Gloria was always a bit whacky, but I had never seen her so vivacious. I found myself getting caught up in her excitement.

"I could have been a singer myself, you know, in my younger days... and Alan plays guitar..."

Sam and Gloria pulled the drum kit out from the garage where it had been huddled up next to Mum's Mitsubishi.

"It's been well looked after," said Gloria. "Just a bit of a rub down and we'll have these cobwebs off. It'll be as good as new."

"Well, have fun, Harriet," said Sam, getting into his car when everything was out on the drive. I waved as he backed out.

"See you tomorrow – nice and early, remember," he called.

"Right then, Miss," said Gloria. "First let's check your chair is on auto. See... I'm starting to get the hang of all this! Now, I'm going to get you a duster. I'll do the washing and you can polish it up."

I went up to the drum kit. I reached out and ran my hand over the cymbal. It was cold. My fingers trailed through the layer of fine dust on the surface. Gloria obviously hoped I'd have Dad's natural ability, but my arms and hands didn't always do what they were told. Would I be any good? I imagined myself on a big tented stage, the crowd roaring their excitement from beyond a blaze of white stage lights as I began my opening routine...

"Here you are, dear," said Gloria, handing me a duster. "You get started over there."

I barely noticed the chill wind on my back as the grey evening became greyer still. Gloria chattered excitedly about the music of her past. I was surprised to find that I knew most of her favourites.

It began to spit rain just as we finished. Gloria looked up from her work.

"Just in time," she said. "Ah, and here's Alan."

The Goldwing grumbled up onto the drive behind me. In Gloria's place in the pillion seat was a guitar in its hard case. There was a big box on the back parcel-shelf.

"What's with this urgent message?" asked Alan, removing his crash helmet and shaking his hair over his shoulders. "Your grandmother sent me a text: COME OVER QUICK AND BRING YOUR ELECTRIC GUITAR. That was all she said. Has she gone doolalay? And where did that drum kit come from?"

"It was in the garage, Alan," said Gloria, reaching up on her tiptoes and planting a deep kiss on his lips. "Help me move it into the house before the heavens let loose. Harriet, you bring in the sticks."

I followed behind Gloria and Alan as they carried the drum kit into the house. Isolated raindrops glittered on the polished steel like diamonds in the hall light.

"Where are we taking it?" asked Alan.

"Straight into Harriet's room," answered Gloria.

Wow! I thought. Jake would be so jealous.

As I lay in bed that night, my mind drifted to the Music room. I had never felt so humiliated in all my life. What if there had been no Charlotte, or no Juliette? Then I thought about Charlotte. Why had she been so late for school? What was wrong with her?

Chapter 24

The first thing I saw the next morning when I opened my eyes was the drum kit, red and black and silver. It made me smile. We'd had fun last night although it was a shame Jake hadn't been around to join in. The old Jake would have helped me and encouraged me. But... things were so different with Mum away. What would Mum say about having the drum kit in my room? She'd never let Jake bring it out of the garage. Maybe Gloria would be able to persuade her to let me keep it. Jake and Andy would come into my room then for their evening jams.

Alan had said to me – "If you can hear the rhythms in your head, it's just a matter of practising." Well practise I would... I got into my chair, pulled my dressing gown over my shoulders and went over to the drums. With a rush of energy, I smashed out a beat. 1, 2 and 3,4 a 5,6,7,8 CRASH! I got it right first time. I tried another one. The sound was crystal clear in my head, but my left hand wouldn't keep up. I tried again and again. I *could* do it.

Gloria touched my shoulder, laughing.

"I said: Come and get your breakfast. There's no time for that. You're going to be ready for Sam this morning, my love."

I put down the sticks and ran my hand over the taut skin of the snare drum. I wished, not for the first time in my life, but more forcefully than usual, that it was Saturday.

The kitchen smelt of sweet floury steam.

"Pancakes, Lovie," said Gloria. "Golden syrup?"

Yes, please.

"No dallying, I really don't want to be late today. We have to prove we can do it."

School! I didn't want to go to school, ever again. The thought made my insides curl. I tried to concentrate on the rich taste of the pancake and the grainy texture of golden syrup, pushing the inevitable approach of school time out of my mind.

"Where's that brother of yours?" asked Gloria, clip-clopping out of the room and up the stairs. "Oo-oo, Jakie... wakey-wakey."

A snake of black smoke wafted out of the frying pan and I began to wonder if I would have to go and rescue it before the whole thing went up in flames.

"Come on, Jakie, you'll be just fine when you get there," said Gloria on her way back down the stairs. "Oh, my goodness, I left a pancake in the pan... well that one will have to go straight in the bin. Are you OK there,

Harriet?" she chuckled. "I can hardly see you with all this smoke. Let me open the window."

Gloria pulled the blind to reveal a very dark, very wet morning.

"There we go, dear, that'll clear it... my, what a nasty morning... That Jake, he doesn't realise, I know all about teenagers and their tricks. He's right as rain. He should just get to bed a little earlier. Fridayitis, that's all it is with him."

I watched my grandmother tossing pancakes and listened to her chat. Did she ever stop talking?

"Right, that's the last of Jake's little pile, I'll pop them in the oven for him. Alan and I will have our breakfast later. I'll go and give your brother another nudge. You go along to your room. I'll be right there..."

We were ready at eight-thirty. Early for the first time since Mum had gone into hospital and on the one morning that I seriously didn't want to go to school.

"Now you wait here in the hall, love," said Gloria at the bottom of the stairs, about to go up to Jake for the eighth time. "Ah, here you are Jakie... Look at you! A bit grey round the edges... Nothing a good night's sleep wouldn't cure my love."

"I'm fine."

"Come and get some breakfast... pancakes. They're nice and hot, I'll just get them out of the oven for you."

"Don't want none," growled Jake, leaning over my chair and grabbing his coat from the peg.

"Come now, you'll feel better after your breakfast."

"I'll be late for school," said Jake, trying to elbow his way past me to get to the front door.

Gloria put her arm in Jake's way, blocking his path and pulled herself up to her full height.

"Now, I insist," she said. "You will have breakfast before you go. You can go in the minibus with Harriet, so you won't be late."

Jake gave Gloria a look and decided to do as she said, but he didn't stop grumbling as he followed her into the kitchen.

"Sit down, my dear. We can't have you going out on an empty stomach. What would your mother say?" Her voice had lost that uncharacteristic harsh tone.

I gazed at the front door. I wished I could ask Gloria if I could stay at home – but going on the Fridayitis comment, there was no point.

A figure loomed in the glass panel in front of me and rang the doorbell. I opened the door.

"Good morning. You look ready."

I smiled half-heartedly.

"Did you have fun with that drum kit last night?" Sam asked.

Yes.

"Good, but why the long face?"

I shrugged.

"Hello there, Sam," said Gloria, tottering out from the kitchen and wiping soap suds from her hands. "Can you take Jake in with you please?"

"I'll walk," Jake shouted from the kitchen.

"You will not walk," the hardness had crept into her voice again, but she winked at me. "It's pouring with rain and you're too late. I can't have that, love – late *and* wet. Now come on, dear, here's your bag." She handed him his schoolbag and he went out into the rain, his head hanging down. "Oh, Jakie," she called.

"What?"

"Take Alan's brolly."

He turned back and snatched the umbrella without looking at Gloria. He put it straight in his bag.

Sam opened the back door of the minibus and got out the ramps.

"Teenagers, hey," he said in an undertone, and winked at me.

We drove to school in silence. Both Jake and I were in very sombre spirits. Rain lashed the windscreen.

"Pull over," said Jake, a few streets from school.

"What do you mean?" asked Sam.

"Just pull over, will you? I'll walk from here."

"OK... Here we are."

Jake let himself out of the van as soon as it had stopped. He slammed the door behind him and hurried into a side alley. As we pulled away, I saw him take a packet of cigarettes from his trouser pocket.

"What's eating him?" asked Sam looking at me in the rear-view mirror. "I hope he's not going to bunk off."

Don't know.

Surely he's not smoking, I thought. But I had seen it with my own eyes.

"Now then, Harry. Are *you* OK?"

Not really.

"You ill?" Sam's eyes searched my face in the mirror.

No.

"What then? Worried about your Mum?"

A bit.

"There's something else... something up at school?"

I made a face.

Sam pulled up outside the school and turned round in his seat to face me.

"Don't worry, Harry. It'll be fine. It's nearly the weekend. Let me know how you get on today, OK? You just let me know..."

I looked up. His eyes met mine.

OK.

"Good girl. Right, I think we're going to have to brave it. Let's be quick or we'll get drenched..."

Chapter 25

I hurried into school, as quickly as my chair would allow, wiping rain from the end of my nose. Charlotte was waiting for me with Thea.

"You're early," said Charlotte. Her voice was flat and very un-Charlotte-like.

I pulled a face, but Charlotte wasn't looking at me.

"Charlotte, please tell me what's going on", said Thea. "I'm your friend, I'm supposed to help you when you've got problems."

We passed under the huge photo of Mr Elliot in the corridor, with his greased down hair and his stern eye. He seemed to be watching me and I remembered my interview with him last spring. We had sat in the Head's clinical-looking office and Mum and Dad took it in turns to pat my hand and grin at me. Mr Elliot carefully explained that it was the first time that someone in a wheelchair had applied to Milton Comprehensive and we must understand that the site was 'split-level', but that we would all have to work together. I felt as if I was on probation. If it didn't work out, I didn't know where I'd go to school. Mum had always refused to talk about it: "You'll fit in, darling. It's a lovely school. It has a good ethos."

"Charlotte?" said Thea.

"There's nothing you can do, Thea," said Charlotte. "Just leave it!"

"Fine!" said Thea. "If that's all you can say then I'll just leave you to it."

She flounced into the girls' toilets.

Crickey! What *was* up with Charlotte? She was always so cheerful.

"Oh no," she groaned. "I can do without Thea going all hissy on me."

We arrived at the form room before the registration bell had sounded and Mrs Jenkins wasn't there yet.

"I'm not in the mood for all this noise," said Charlotte holding the door open.

"Hawwo Hawwiet. How was Zyborg?" taunted Greg even before I had reached my desk.

"Shut up," snapped Juliette.

"Ooooh touchy!" sneered Trescott. "There should be a law against sticking up for aliens – but then you're an alien too, aren't you, Juliette?"

"That's right. We've got two aliens on our table. We'll have to make a formal complaint."

"Or annihilate them ourselves."

I wished I could be invisible.

"What's going on?" asked Charlotte, coming up behind me.

"We were just wondering what to do about having two aliens on our table." Trescott leaned forward, enjoying his game.

"Yeh, we might get infected – our minds taken over by unknown forces," said Greg.

"Are you sure you haven't been taken over already? If not, then I think it would be a definite improvement," returned Charlotte.

"Oooh!" said Greg.

"Just cut it out, OK?" said Charlotte.

"Who's gonna make me?" asked Greg.

"You just remember... I know stuff about you..." There was a pointed threat in her voice.

Greg hesitated and he blushed violently. I wondered what Charlotte knew about Greg that he was so worried about.

*

All morning, it seemed like the boys were making fun of my voice; in the corridors, in undertones in lessons. The walls seemed to echo with the monstrous sound of my voice. Even some of the nicer boys were looking at me strangely, with their tongues pushing out their bottom lips. The girls were more subtle, but most of *them* were walking round my chair in wider circles than usual.

However Charlotte's threat related to Greg, at least *he* seemed to be keeping his mouth shut. But it didn't stop him casting resentful and sarcastic looks at me all the time.

I was worried about Charlotte. Whenever I glanced at her during lessons, she seemed lost in her own world... sad.

Chapter 26

I spent most of break time and lunchtime in the disabled loo, avoiding everyone. The bell sounded for afternoon registration and I reluctantly left my safe haven. I nearly collided with Anna Simpson who was in my class at primary school. Anna turned red and moved out of the way, but then she put her hand on my shoulder.

"You OK, Harriet?" she asked. "I heard about what happened yesterday. I wish I'd been there. I'd have put that Gregory Peterson in his place. He's a nasty piece of work, that one."

Thanks!

So, the news had officially spread throughout Year 7. Great.

I found Charlotte waiting for me outside the form room with Juliette.

"Hi, Harriet, where've you been? We were looking for you."

I shrugged and made my way to my desk, careful that I didn't look at anyone. I didn't need to attract any attention. A small corner of my heart felt thrilled that Charlotte and

Juliette had wanted to spend time with me at lunch.

Miss Jenkins marched into the room, her face purple.

"Silence, 7G," she bellowed. For a short woman, she had a loud voice and incredible authority. The class fell quiet immediately. "I have just spoken to Mr Jones. I have to say that I am ashamed of you – all of you. What do you think you were playing at, causing all that disruption? When the teacher leaves the room, you are expected to be on your VERY BEST behaviour. You are a disgrace, 7G. Acting like pre-schoolers…"

I twisted my little finger in a hole in my tights and watched the ladder creep down my leg.

At last the bell sounded.

"…and I'll have no more of it," finished Miss Jenkins. "Any changes to the register? No? Well, off you go to Year 7 assembly. Be warned, I shall be checking up on you from now on. Harriet, if you could wait behind for one moment."

I waited for the class to leave. Charlotte hovered by the door.

"You're OK, Charlotte. Come in and close the door. Now, Harriet, I gather you were at the centre of this fiasco yesterday." Miss Jenkins smiled sadly at me. Tears pricked my eyes and I looked at the floor. "As Mr Jones described events to me, you started all the uproar by shouting at one of the boys. Now Harriet. How do you expect the class to react to you? You never speak to anyone – although your records quite clearly state that you can speak if you want to – and then you shout out at the top of your voice? It's no wonder your classmates responded as they did, is it, dear?"

A tear trickled down my cheek. I looked at Miss Jenkins trying to read her. Her voice was so kind, as though butter wouldn't melt, but I felt thoroughly told off.

"But Miss," said Charlotte. "It wasn't like that. It was Greg, Miss, he's been teasing Harriet really badly this week…"

"Yes, well we all know what Gregory Peterson can be like. Harriet, I have noticed that things have been really slipping for you – yes, and maybe the teasing is on the increase. Do you think I should speak to your parents… let them know how difficult things are getting for you here? Maybe it's time you thought about going to another school? I'm not really sure that Milton Comprehensive is the right place…"

I gazed at the floor through tears which threatened to tumble uncontrollably. Unchecked, they would cascade like rivers down my face and flow and flow until I drowned.

"Harriet?"

I gazed at the pencil shavings on Miss Jenkins' desk and shrugged. What could I possibly say? It was true; I never wanted to wheel my chair through the doors of Milton Comp again. But why would anywhere else be any different?

"So, Charlotte," said Miss Jenkins, having obviously finished with me. "How are you coping?"

"I'm fine."

"You know, if you need time off…"

"I'm fine," she didn't look fine. Her face was closed. She wasn't going to say anything to Miss Jenkins who looked disappointed.

"You're right. It's best to keep everything as normal as possible."

"Yeah, right Miss."

"Still, you've got good friends, haven't you?" She picked up her board rubber.

"Yes, Miss."

"Ok then, off you go to assembly, girls. You're late," she said, turning to the whiteboard.

From the way Charlotte stomped down the corridor I could see she was angry.

"In here," she said, holding open the door of the girls' loos.

There was a mixture of pungent smells in the girls' loos, including, I thought, cigarettes. A large frosted window faced over the field. Unfortunately, it was bolted shut.

"That woman is totally out of order, she really is. Are you OK, Harriet?"

I shook my head and the tears spilled over.

"I can't believe she spoke to you like that. It's outrageous. None of this is your fault, Harriet, it really isn't."

I hunched my back and all the emotion of the last week tumbled out. The tears fell until my skirt felt damp. Charlotte rubbed my back.

"It's all right," she said. "Let it all out."

The bell sounded for afternoon lessons and I went over to the sinks and washed my face. I was relieved that the mirror was too high up to see into. I didn't want to see how blotchy my face was and how red my eyes.

"Well at least we've got Greg off your case for a bit," said Charlotte passing a paper towel.

I dried my eyes and gave Charlotte a questioning look.

"Oh, I know lots of stories about him – his mum and... mine... are... good friends." Now Charlotte's eyes clouded over.

I reached my hand out and mustered my clearest voice. "You OK?"

"Yeah, but that Miss Jenkins has got to be stupid. Some things are so massive they turn everything upside-down and nothing will ever be the same again."

Chapter 27

"So, how was your day then?" said Sam as he climbed into the car that evening.

I did the 'so-so' movement with my hand, tilting it from side to side. I couldn't even begin to explain how wearing the constant taunting was, let alone Miss Jenkins' attitude.

"So, not as bad as yesterday, then?"

No.

"OK, as long as you know you can tell me anything..."

Yes. He was so nice.

Sam was off, chatting about his planned weekend with Evette. He was really excited.

I was relieved as we drove out of the school gates at the thought of two whole days without the agro. I couldn't wait to get on the drum kit and bang out all my frustration.

As we stopped at the traffic lights near the park, I watched a toddler in a pushchair. He was pointing at the swings through the hedge and waggling his little legs about, his face puce with rage. I remembered how much I had loved the swings when I was small enough to be lifted in and out and how Jake would push me really high until my stomach flew into the treetops and made me laugh.

Jake... me and Jake really needed to talk. He was the only one who would understand how I felt – about Mum... and Gloria... and Dad, going off right now, with Mum in hospital and everything. And maybe he'd have heard about what happened in the Music room.

Gloria ushered me into the house as soon as I got home.

"Ooh, let's get you in out of sight of that nosy parker over there. Why she can't just mind her own business... No, no, you come on in the kitchen, dear. I want to see what homework you've got. Now you didn't tell me you get homework..." She waggled her finger. "I had to hear it from that nice Mrs Alcott... Hot chocolate?"

Yes please.

"Me too, I think. Now you get your stuff out and show me what you've got to do."

I was surprised to find how helpful Gloria was.

"This takes me back," said Gloria as I copied my English up in neat as best I could. "I bet you didn't know I was a Classroom Assistant when your father was in his teens?"

The motorbike revved out on the drive.

"Ah, here's Alan already. I'd better think about dinner. Have you finished that now? So, you've just got that computer homework?"

She said, going over to the little mirror on top of the fridge. "Well, don't ask for any help with that! I'm an old bird, me." She paused while she dragged scarlet lipstick round her open mouth. "Can't teach an old dog new tricks is what they say." She rubbed her lips together and blotted them on a piece of kitchen towel. "That's better. Now make sure you get that homework done before you do anything else."

I turned on the computer. How did it take eleven years for my grandmother to start talking to me like a real person? I opened Outlook. We had to send an email to someone in the class. They were private, Miss Porter had said, so she wouldn't be reading the contents, just checking they had been sent. There was one new message, from school, with a list of the school addresses of all the other kids in the class. Looking at all the names on the list there was only one person I really wanted to send an email to. I added Charlotte to my address book and sat back. What should I say? I started typing...

Hi Charlotte, I'm glad we had this homework today. I really wanted to say thank you to you for being so nice to me this week. I'm sorry to be such a burden when you obviously have enough to think about. Look, you don't have to say anything if you don't want to... but if you wanted someone to talk to... well, you already know I won't say a word to anyone!

I read over the message and then, worrying that the last sentence was too nosy, I highlighted it and my hand hovered over the delete button. But maybe it would help Charlotte to talk about things. I knew I wished *I* could talk to someone about my troubles sometimes. I typed my name and pressed the send button. Charlotte could just ignore the last bit if she wanted to, but at least I'd made the offer.

I looked in my inbox again. I was disappointed to find that there were no other new messages. I had thought my aunt would have responded by now... unless she was on her way from South Africa. But no, she wouldn't really be able to arrange things that quickly and she would at least have phoned.

Looking at the list of addresses from school I decided to email Juliette. She'd been nice to me too.

The doorbell sang out its stupid song as I turned off the computer and I went to investigate.

Alan was at the door taking two huge carrier bags from a delivery boy in a green stripy uniform.

"Ah," he said, spotting me as he closed the door. "Good, dinner's up!" I wondered if his smile would crack his face in two. "Ever had Chinese?"

I shook my head.

"Come on through then. We're eating in the sitting room. I've hired some DVDs. Your choice."

There was so much food. The dishes were colourful, and the smells were tangy but mouth-watering: lemon and syrup and spices.

"Tuck in, girlie," said Alan, grinning.

The phone rang.

"Typical," said Gloria resting her plate on the coffee table and tottering out.

"OK, Jake... Yes... I suppose so. Well OK, but I'd like you back by 5 on Sunday."

She put the phone down and came back.

"He'll be home late tonight and then he wants to go back over to his friend's tomorrow and stay the night. We'd be no company for him, would we? Press play, love."

Alan had managed to find a film I'd never seen before about a beautiful Chinese girl who had to pretend to be a boy and go to war in place of her father. What a great film! I knew only too well what it's like to feel you have been put in the wrong body and to have people look at you and assume they know what you are capable of. I got really carried away by the story. Just once, looking over at the sofa where Gloria sat with the lights from the screen flickering on her face and her legs curled up beside her, I wished that I was snuggled up there, all cosy, between Mum and Jake, like normal.

Chapter 28

The next morning dawned bright and crisp. A weekend without Mum! A first. Did Gloria know that I had horse riding on a Saturday? The smell of bacon filtered out of the kitchen. I put on my dressing-gown and went to investigate.

"Hello, dear. Ready for breakfast?" Gloria obviously hadn't looked in the mirror yet. Yesterday's mascara was heavily smudged around her eyes. I'm sure *she* was crying at the film too.

"Mmm," I said. *That smells good.*

Alan sat at the table his yellow nicotine-stained fingers laced around a mug of coffee. He wore paisley pyjamas under a corduroy robe, the ever-present cravat still at his throat. He grinned at me.

"So then, Miss. You're off to the hairdressers with your grandma, and I'm checkin' out me horses," he winked. "Then we'll go an' see yer Mum?"

Yes – but...

"Don't you worry your little heart, love."

"She's on the mend, dear, you'll see," said Gloria, putting two plates on the table with a flourish.

"You not eating, Pumpkin?"

"Oh, yes, I've opened a tin of grapefruit for myself. After last night's binge, I'd better go careful. Got to watch my figure." She patted her stomach through her pyjamas. There was nothing of her.

I glanced at the clock, the one that Dad brought back from Vienna on one of his many business trips. Nine-thirty.

"I got horse riding today," I said.

"Eer hor – horse riding?" said Gloria, a spoonful of fruit hovering in front of her mouth. "What time?"

"Eleven-thirty."

"That should be fine... we can fit it in after the hairdressers."

"Where do you go?" said Alan, through a mouthful of sausage.

I pointed to the leaflet on the notice board.

*

But Gloria forgot about the horse riding. It didn't take much.

We were met at the door of the hairdressers by Michael, a tall man with not a hair on his head and black eye-liner framing his huge emerald eyes. He wore a black silk shirt and trousers pinched in tight at the waist with a diamond-studded belt.

"Gloria, darling! It's simply heaven to see you. And who is this?"

"This, my gem, is Harriet."

"An honour to meet you," said Michael, with a bow. "Let's settle you down in the waiting area while we get Gloria all primmied up." He turned to Gloria, "Now then, Gloria. Darling, you're in for a trim and touch up. But, let me see..." He lifted her hair away from her head and ran it through his fingers. "Yes, I think so... It's time for a fresh set and don't you think some peach highlights, ready for the new season?"

"Oh! Do you think so, my gem? Well, it has been getting a little difficult to manage... yes, and a bit tired-looking. Peach, you say?"

"Oh, darling, yes! Will lift it no end and accentuate the colour of your cheeks."

I watched them for a while as Michael danced around my grandmother, then paused, one hand on his hip, the other under his chin, head on one side. He'd keep the pose for a moment, then was off on his gig again to view her from another angle. I could see why Gloria liked him so much. His attention was absolute.

I flicked though the magazines on the faux leather coffee table. *'How to look amazing this spring'; 'Food to warm you to your toes'; 'I keep getting hot flushes, is this the menopause?'.*

My stars said: '*If the days ahead look long and dark, you should not give up hope, you will find the answers within yourself.*'

Yeh, right!

The clock ticked and time passed. At 11.35, Gloria finally stood up.

"Oh, it looks magnificent; I never would have believed it. You are such a gem, Michael."

"But darling, don't forget. You really must use this 'extreme moisture', once a week, twice if possible... pop it on and wrap your head in a warm towel for twenty minutes. It's as easy as that."

Gloria caught sight of my face.

"Harriet, love, what is the matter?" she exclaimed. She followed my eyes to the clock. "Oh no, dear, I'm so sorry. Michael, I clean forgot her riding lesson. She's missed it now!"

"Sweetie, that will never do! How can we bring that smile back to her little face?"

"Michael, my gem... could you do me an enormous favour and cut her hair? You do it so nicely, I'm sure she'd love it."

"For you, darling, anything! My next lady is not due for half an hour," he said in his lilting sing-song voice. "Sweetie, may I ask for the honour of cutting your hair?"

I had to giggle as Michael made a sweeping curtsey and held out his hands.

Mum always cut my hair in the bath with a ruler and a pair of dressmaking scissors, but today I had my hair washed backwards in a basin with a hole cut out for my neck. They had to remove the back of my chair for that, but they didn't make me feel awkward about it – *'lots of my ladies come in chairs,'* so Michael said.

Michael stood behind me and together we looked into the mirror. My hair trailed damp well past my shoulders. He combed it lovingly. Now *I* was his darling.

"Let's layer it down. Do you want to keep the length?"

I held my breath and shook my head. Mum would go mad!

By the time I came out of the hairdresser's, I felt like a queen. My hair was so well thinned that it didn't feel like mine anymore and we had ceremonially binned the hair bobble and clips. I wouldn't be needing *them* anymore.

*

When we got back to the house to pick up Jake, he had already gone out, so it was just me, Gloria and Alan who stood beside the nurses' desk waiting for the over-large sister to look up from her keyboard.

"Mrs Harris," she snapped, eyeing us with her piggy eyes. "Second door on the left. Don't stay too long, she needs her rest."

Bet she loves saying that to people. Like an old-fashioned matron.

The sister stuffed half a Mars bar into her mouth and chewed, her mean eyes following us.

It was a hot, airless ward steeped in the cloying smell of milk and draped in a fine shroud of talcum powder. Further up the corridor was an odd cawing noise which sounded like a seagull but must have been the mew of a newborn baby.

"Helloee, how's the patient today?" said Gloria opening the door to Mum's side-room. "Look who we've brought to see you."

I hesitated and looked at Alan who was awkwardly holding the bunch of anemones I had chosen at the market.

"In you go then," he said ruffling my hair.

I edged forwards, plastering a big Gloria-style smile on my face. Mum was in bed with a Sudoku puzzle book over her knee. A wire came up from under the covers and was hooked up to a grey monster on wheels beside the bed which made the beep-beep-beep of a heart-beat. A drip fed a clear liquid into Mum's left arm. The whole room was reminiscent of the death-bed scenes on TV, but Mum looked quite relaxed, if a little green. The acid smell of vomit lingered in the air.

"Alan, can you go and get a nurse to take that away?" she said indicating a grey cardboard tray on her bedside table. "You'd better get them to bring another one. I don't know if it's the pregnancy or just the food in this place. I've never been so sick in all my life…"

Alan looked pleased to have an excuse to leave the room.

"Harriet! Your hair! You look so… grown up?"

"Like it?" I held my breath.

"Well… I wouldn't have done it… but – it looks really great."

I flashed a proper smile.

"Do I see your influence here, Gloria?"

"I took her to the hairdressers, but I left it to her what she had done. I didn't really think, pet. You're not too upset, are you?"

"No, not at all. A proper hair cut was long overdue. I tend to baby her a bit too much I suppose," said Mum, smiling affectionately at me. "I'm glad it was something for you two to enjoy together…" her voice drifted off. She looked around the room. "Where's Jake?"

"Oh, you know boys," said Gloria. "He's off out seeing his friends."

Mum looked concerned. "Is he OK?"

"Don't worry, pet, he's fine isn't he Harriet?"

I nodded, looking sideways at Gloria.

Alan returned with a nurse and a vase for the flowers. He stationed himself behind me, his hand resting on my shoulder. I was pleased by the support. Mum told us the baby was due in the middle of August, which was, according to Gloria, much sooner than expected.

"You must keep well rested though, dear," said Gloria.

"I know." Mum looked anxious.

"At least Anthony will be back in a few weeks to help."

"Oh, yes, he is very good," said Mum.

Except when he deserts us in our hour of need, I thought.

We stayed for about half-an-hour before the Sister waddled in and shooed us away. I was relieved to go. It was hard to think of things to say in this alien environment.

"I hate hospitals," said Alan as the door of the ward shut behind us. It was the first time he had spoken since we had arrived.

Chapter 29

The house was quiet when I woke up the next morning. It took a while to work out why my arms ached so much: it was all that drumming yesterday afternoon. I rubbed my biceps and wondered if Charlotte had responded to my email. Curiosity finally drove me out from underneath the warm duvet and I switched on the computer and went to the bathroom while it warmed up. My hair was stuck up on one side, so I wet my hairbrush and ran it through. It was great – I could manage it myself! I threaded my fingers through the ends and scrunched in some of my new mousse like *The Gem* had shown me yesterday. It looked *fab!*

There were three new messages in my inbox. The first was from Greg:

Hello Harriet. Don't forget I'm always more than happy to help you out anytime your battery conks out.

He was crafty. There wasn't much anyone could say about that, but he was just gloating about making me shout at him. I right-clicked and deleted the message.

The next email was from Charlotte.

Hi Harriet.

Of course I'll stick up for you, no matter what. It's wrong, some of the things people say.

I don't know if I should tell you what is going on. I want to tell you, but then again, I don't want anyone to know. No one would understand. It's just awful. I can't believe it. My dad can't believe it. We thought everything was fine. Yes, Mum had post-natal depression after Skye was born, but we thought that was all over. Skye's my baby sister – well, half-sister, so it turns out. There. That's it. I've said it. All along Dad... we assumed Skye was his baby. But Mum's been seeing this guy Steve for years it turns out. Can you believe it? Steve is 25! Ten years younger than Mum. He's one of Dad's workmates, like a friend. Some friend. It's just stupid. It's the kind of thing that happens on TV not in real life. Anyway, Mum's left to go and live with Steve. And... unreal... she's taken Skye with her. My little Skye. Well. I don't know if I can send this. I mean... like you don't need my hassle. But I do need to tell someone. And Thea and that wouldn't help. They'd be talking about it all the time... going on about it. Slagging my Mum off – saying my Dad didn't pay her enough attention... I just don't want them to

149

know. It's so embarrassing. I don't know. I'm gonna send this anyway. It would be good if just one person knew how I felt – other than Dad. I can't talk to Dad. I've never seen him like this. It's like she died. The doctor's put him on medication.
Well. Here goes. I'm sending,
Charlotte.

I leaned back in my chair. And I thought I had problems! Poor Charlotte!

The last email was from Charlotte as well:

Harriet, I answered your question. I've got one for you. You don't have to answer if you don't want to but why do you live with your grandmother?
Charlotte

I wondered how Charlotte knew about Gloria. As I tried to decide what I could tell her, there was a knock at the door. It was Alan's face that poked round the crack.

"Good, you're up. I've got a trip planned. We're going out."

Where to?

He tapped the end of his crocked nose and winked. "Wait and see," he said mysteriously. "Get some warm clothes on and come and get breakfast. I'll go and put the kettle on. Gloria will be in in a minute to give you a hand."

Breakfast was pain au chocolat from the supermarket – apparently Sunday's meals were Alan's responsibility. Then Alan helped me into Mum's car and bundled the chair in the boot.

"Come on, my love, out with it. Where are we going?" asked Gloria making big eyes at Alan as he got into the driving seat.

"Now petal, you know I'll never say. Just sit back and enjoy the ride."

As we drove past the road that led to the hospital, I gazed down it wistfully. It was a shame that Mum couldn't come with us on this mystery journey. The morning had dawned bright and sunny, but the wind still held more than a hint of winter.

We sped out into the countryside. Daffodils dotted the hedgerows, but the trees and bushes held tight to their buds. It had been a long hard winter and the recent rainfall had been only a few degrees off freezing. Spring seemed slow in coming.

The familiar villages, with their little stone cottages, became fewer and further between until we went over a cattle grid into the grey wasteland of the moors. Odd clusters of sheep scrabbled for the last remaining scraps of grass. The hay put out by the farmers had been blown up into the scraggy trees, useless to the hungry livestock. They seemed to be watching the horizon to the south, as though searching for signs of a warmer spell of weather coming their way with the sunshine.

Alan suddenly veered off the road and down a track that looked as though it led to nowhere. The road became more and more potholed as we continued along it. Alan reached forward to switch on the CD player and The Three Tenors pounded out at full volume. This certainly wasn't Mum's music.

Gloria looked back at me. "Full of surprises this one, eh – I bet you didn't know he had a secret passion for Opera?"

I shook my head, smiling.

Alan turned the heaters up and opened the windows. His hair streamed manically behind him.

"You getting in the mood?" he asked, turning to look at me, grinning his brown-toothed smile.

The track swung to the right round an outcrop of rocks. We raced round the corner, scattering sheep in all directions with Gloria laughing and singing along to the music. Surely these two were far too old for these kinds of shenanigans.

The road opened out into a parking area and Alan skidded the car to a halt.

"Wow, Alan," gasped Gloria. "How do you find these places?"

The view was truly stunning. The scraggy cliffs and harsh stone of the moors dropped away revealing the costal basin and the river meandering majestically on its path. In the distance, the sun sparkled jewel-like on the sea.

"Do you mind if Gloria and I stretch our legs?" asked Alan, craning his head into the back. "We won't go out of sight."

No problem.

"Let's leave the windows down so you get to enjoy the breeze. I've got a blanket in the boot for you."

Alan and Gloria walked to the edge of the moor, where the landscape plummeted out of sight, Gloria struggling slightly in her heeled boots. They held hands which they swung between them. Gloria was lucky to be so much in love at her age. I thought about Charlotte's news. It was funny how both of us had lost our mums recently, although in different circumstances. With Charlotte's mum, there would be guilt and shame, disappointment and blame. At least with my mum, the hurt was through bad luck pure and simple. Poor Charlotte, what a horrible situation to be in.

Gloria and Alan came running up to the car laughing and flung open the doors.

"This man is terrible," said Gloria climbing in and banging the door shut. "He really should at least tell me what to wear on these expeditions of his. He just thinks it's a joke."

"Brrr, that's chilly," said Alan getting in.

"I'm saying you should warn me what to wear on my feet. These are my brand-new boots. I thought we were going shopping."

"What is it with women and shopping?" said Alan with a chuckle reaching behind his seat for the cool box. "I told you to wear your warmest, most sensible clothes. What more could I do?"

"You just think it's funny, you toad," Gloria chided. "What's for lunch then Mister?"

"Sandwiches, courtesy of the Co-op. Harriet, egg or cheese and ham?"

We ate sandwiches, crisps and chocolate biscuits and sipped mugs of scalding hot tea from a thermos. Then Alan scrunched all the rubbish into a plastic bag, stuffing it in the cool box and we set off again. Back at the main road, Alan turned left towards the sea. I felt the mounting excitement I always felt when we were going to the seaside. It never mattered what time of year it was, the coast was always exhilarating. We parked up in the little village of Bishop's Post where a handful of parking spaces huddled by the sea, opposite a fish restaurant and a curio shop. Ours was the only car.

Alan helped me into my chair and wrapped the blanket round my legs. The noise of the crashing waves filled my ears making me want to laugh and dance and sing. I contented myself with a big grin as the salty wind, which whistled horizontal off the sea, did its best to mess up my new hair style. We set off along the seafront. Bishop's Post consisted of about two dozen cottages lined up against the shoreline, a narrow road running in front of them. It was high tide, so there was no sign of the beach. The footpath doubled as the sea wall and dropped straight into the frothing water below. A rusty iron railing was all that separated pedestrians from the foaming sea.

My chair went faster than Alan and Gloria, and the pavement was narrow, so I went on ahead. The sun was beginning to dip low in the sky. Perfect timing for seeing mermaids, I mused, scanning the horizon. The wind whistled and the waves crashed against the sea wall just a few feet from my wheels. I imagined living in one of the little cottages, watching gulls playing in the wind, running (wouldn't that be a dream come true?) across the sand at low tide with Jake and my new brother or sister, finding starfish and crabs in the rock pools. *If only.*

I heard a whistle behind me and turned my chair. I had gone quite a long way in front of Alan and Gloria. They were signalling for me to come back.

"Come and watch the sunset," said Alan, as I joined them, pointing out over the sea.

I faced the sea and leaned forward over the railing, the wind whipping around my ears. I remembered what Dad used to say when I was small, "If you listen very carefully, you'll hear the hiss as the sun touches the water." I had always got really quiet, listening hard.

In the middle distance, I saw a jet of water shoot into the air. I grabbed Gloria's hand and pointed as a large grey body slid majestically out of the sea, hovered, and came back down with a crash.

"A whale!" exclaimed Gloria. "Alan, did you see? Was that really a whale? I've never seen a whale before."

All noise, all movement seemed to cease. We stood, straining our eyes in the mounting darkness. Against all odds, we were standing here, me and Gloria and Alan, looking out to sea at the very time this great beast went past. Where was it going? Where had it come from? This was better than magic; it was real.

The moment passed and was gone with the whale.

Gloria shivered.

"Fish and chips," said Alan, pulling Gloria close and rubbing his hand up and down her shoulder.

There were two steps into the restaurant to keep out the floods when the sea level got too high so I had to wait outside. We ate in the car as the light drained out of the day as if being sucked down an invisible plughole.

The fresh air had made me sleepy and I dozed on the way back. When I opened my eyes, we were home. The house was in darkness.

"That brother of yours! He should have been home by now," groaned Gloria.

"I'll have a word with him, petal. Don't worry," said Alan.

"Right then, love," said Gloria as we pulled our coats off in the hall. "We're going to have to give you a bath. You're getting smelly!"

I gave Gloria a wide-eyed look.

"I'm joking – but you will if we don't do the deed."

It could have been awkward, but Gloria kept me covered up with a towel as much as possible, saying it was to stop me getting cold and then she put candles around the bath and turned out the main light. She brought in the portable radio and found the jazz channel and left me to soak in a hot bath that smelled of lavender.

While I was in the bath, Jake came home. It sounded as though he and Alan were having a row.

"I'll do what I want," shouted Jake as he stomped upstairs.

I had one last job to do before I went to bed. I went back to my computer and typed out a reply to Charlotte.

Charlotte,
I am so sorry to hear about your news. My problems seem small compared to what you must be going through at the moment. There's

not much I can do. But I can promise to keep shtum.

In answer to your question. I don't normally live with my grandma – by the way, how did you know? My grandma has come to look after us. My dad's away on business and Mum's in hospital. She's pregnant but everything isn't right. It's funny, when Mum went in, it felt like the worst thing ever was having my grandmother here. But it turns out she's pretty cool.

Harriet.

I pressed send. I actually wished I had an email in my inbox from Dad even though I was still a bit cross with him.

As I was falling asleep, I wondered what Jake was getting up to when he was out of the house. He and Cameron hadn't seemed to have that much in common until last week. Now they were as thick as thieves.

Chapter 30

I woke up the next morning feeling fuzzy-headed. There was something I had to remember, a dream that had been playing round in my head all night: something about Jake, something important.

I shook my head and rubbed my eyes. If it was that important, it would come to me.

Jake was up, but he looked grey and tired at the kitchen table and he was arguing with Gloria.

"You can't take time off school just because you've been living it up too much at the weekend, dear. This is an important year for you. You've got your 'O' levels coming up."

"GCSE s and they're not till next year."

"Even so," said Gloria firmly, placing a bowl of porridge in front of him, "this'll perk you up. I bet you didn't eat properly at your friend's house." She glanced at me, "Brown sugar, love?"

Yes.

Gloria was already dressed in her tight jeans and leopard-skin wrap around. She liked to show off her figure. I had to admit she looked good for a granny – if a bit over-the-top.

*

Sam was grinning from ear to ear when he came to pick me up.

"Hey-yup, Harry. How's you?"

I did the 'so-so' hand waggle. Actually, when I thought about it, I wasn't dreading school as much as I could have been. Yes, there would be the teasing, but I'd had that for six months and it hadn't killed me yet. But I sort-of, almost had a friend. I wondered if that was how Charlotte would think of me. A friend. Maybe. After all, she'd told me a secret she didn't want anyone else to know.

"Where's your plaits?!" asked Sam.

I beamed.

"Mighty Jo! You look swell. You've got a good hairdresser there."

Sam fiddled with the radio. The sunshine had disappeared along with the weekend, but at least it wasn't raining.

"Mum not back then?"

No.

"Did you see her though?"

Yes. But she didn't look good.

The traffic was very heavy, and we had come to a standstill.

"What's up with her? Your grandmother just said she was in hospital," asked Sam, turning round in his seat.

I mimed a pregnant tummy with my hand.

"She's having a baby?"

Yes.

"Wow!"

The car behind honked its horn impatiently and Sam went back to his driving.

"They're so good nowadays, hospitals. It's amazing what they can do. She's in the best place... But other than that, you had a good weekend?"

I nodded in the rear-view mirror.

"You?" I asked.

"Harry! You wouldn't believe it. It's like Evette and I... well it sounds corny but it's like we were just made for each other."

I smiled. He radiated a kind of energy and happiness that was new for him.

"It's weird, man. I've never felt like this before. We've spent the whole weekend just... you know... drinking coffee and talking. Evette! She could talk for Europe and she's so funny."

You're in love!

"Hey – is that Jake?" asked Sam as we turned into the school.

Jake was heading the wrong way – out of the school gates, his hands in his pockets and his head dangling to one side as though it had grown too heavy.

"He doesn't look right these days, does he?"

I shook my head.

*

"Your hair!" said Charlotte in reception. "Turn around."

I swivelled my chair to show Charlotte the back.

"Wow – that's so groovy! What an improvement. Was it your grandmother's idea?"

Yes.

"Cool!"

How did you know?

"How did I know about her? Alice said your taxi driver was going to talk to your grandmother – that day your battery died? We thought it was a bit odd."

There was a strong smell of disinfectant. The caretaker was in the corridor with a mop and bucket, a short man, with ginger hair sticking out from under a checked flat-cap. Everyone called him Basil, but I don't think that was really his name.

"Ah, Harriet," – why can't I be anonymous, like everyone else? – "wait there with yer friend. I won't be long. We don't want this mess on yer tyres... It was yer brother what did it. Threw 'is breakfast all over... Err boys!" he said, raising his voice as three Year 11s pushed past Charlotte and me. "You blind? Can't ya see the cone? Either wait or go round the other way."

The lads laughed at him and picked their way over the porridgy goo, saying "Yuck!" and "Gross out!"

Basil shook his fists at their backs, his ginger tendrils trembling. "I should make yerall come back and mop irrup yerselves."

"Yer, right!" they called.

∗

"I know it's in here somewhere," said Charlotte rummaging through her bag after our French lesson. "It has to be."

"Catch us up," said Alice, disappearing into the corridor after Thea and Codey.

"This is crazy. I got an extension on my French homework as it is, so I have to hand it in today. I know it's in here." She was becoming quite upset.

"Bring it down to the staff room, Charlotte," said the stick insect in her lilting French-accented English.

"Yes, Miss. I'll find it..." She emptied out her bag on the table in front of her. I hovered by her side, waiting. "Here, can you hold these?"

Charlotte handed me a fluffy pink pencil-case, a calculator and something else that looked like a calculator but had letters instead of numbers. I turned it on.

'hello' I typed.

'my name is harriet'

I looked at it. This could mean...

'how was your weekend' I wrote.

"At last! Why did I put it in my notebook?" said Charlotte as she replaced her books tidily in her bag. She held out her hand and I passed her the pencil case and calculator.

"I'm losing it! Now, where's my spellchecker?"

I touched her arm and showed her the message.

"My weekend?" Her mouth dropped open. "Harriet, this is brilliant, why didn't I think of it?"

Now I was doing a totally batty Alan-style grin. It was as though a door had been opened to reveal a whole new world, where I could actually say things without speaking.

"Well… My weekend was really odd. Dad's so quiet – the whole house is quiet, without Skye. You don't realise how much noise toddlers make until they're gone…" She put her bag on her back and picked up the French homework.

"When did you find out about your Mum?" she asked as we went out of French Two.

'last monday' I typed.

"So, when's it due?"

'16th August'

"Did you see her at the weekend?"

Yes. The corridor was packed. This was the time that I usually dreaded – heckling from the other students at break time and lunch time. But if anyone was saying anything, I didn't hear them, I was too busy.

"How was she?"

'dunno it was scary' The excitement tingled inside me. I wouldn't have even tried to have this conversation if I had to speak.

Charlotte knocked on the staff room door and a very tall teacher I didn't recognise opened it. He had the wrinkles of a thousand frowns on his face.

"What d'you want?" he growled.

"Can you give this to Mme Lefage, please, Sir?" said Charlotte.

She giggled as he shut the door.

"He looked like Worf off *Star Trek*. What subject does he teach?"

I shrugged and showed Charlotte the spellchecker.

'mum had this thing strapped to her tummy to measure her heartbeat'

Charlotte laughed as she read the message.

"Don't worry, that's the baby's heart-beat. They always put that thing on. It doesn't mean anything. How did you get on with that English homework?"

I was surprised when the bell went for PE. We had been chatting all through break and I hadn't even thought of hiding in the loo.

*

It was drizzling again at the end of school and Charlotte had left me in the main entrance to wait for Sam. I saw him pull into the car park and went to the front door to find that the exit was blocked by two boys. They could see me, but they just stood there, finishing their conversation. I waited.

I need to get out, I glared.

"We've got the cripple here, waiting to go," said the one with the acne explosion all over his face.

"OK," said the other. "Well, see ya tomorrow... let me know about Friday."

They finally cleared out of the way.

*

Jake wasn't in when I got home, and Gloria was hopping mad.

"He was sent home sick today. Prowling the house like a caged lion, getting in my way. Moody so and so, isn't he? Well, you can't just up and out when you've had a day off sick. It's not right. I know things are hard for him, but he shouldn't take it out on the rest of us..." She stopped and looked down at me "I'm sorry, dear, I know it isn't your fault. I'll stop going on about it now. Can I get you a drink?"

Jake was back before dinner looking much better. He even stayed in for most of the evening listening to music in his bedroom.

Chapter 31

Jake was all alone at Bishop's Post. He was strapped into my wheelchair. It was dark. He watched a storm brewing up fast from the belly of the sea. The wind dragged his hair back from his face. A vacant face. A hollow face. Black tears of blood fell from his eyes and pooled on his knees. A flash lit up the sky and I could see that the railing had gone. The sea crashed over the sea wall onto the pavement, swirling a white froth around the wheels of the chair like lacy tentacles enticing him into the sea to be devoured by the waves. Jake's hand was on the knob. The veins of his hand shone luminous through his skin and the thunder roared.

I woke in a cold sweat.

Chapter 32

Mrs Alcott was away that morning, taking her son to Fracture Clinic, according to Miss Jenkins. So, at 11.30, it was Charlotte who stood with me outside the office where the School Councillor normally held her clinics.

"Shall I wait out here for you?"

No, come in. I pointed at the door.

"You want me to come in?"

Yes, why not.

A mousey haired woman I'm sure I'd never seen before opened the door, smiling. I'd had so many Speech Therapists over the years, all of them non-descript and none of them lasting more than a term.

"Come on in," said the Speech Therapist and retreated into the stuffy little room, positioning herself behind a coffee table. She didn't give her name.

She looked up as Charlotte followed me into the room. "Do you want to wait outside?"

"Well, I could, but Harriet said she wanted me to come in with her."

"Is that OK, Harriet?"

I nodded.

"I don't see why not. There's a chair over there by the door."

"So, how are you getting on, Harriet?"

I made a face.

"Right, we need to do a follow-up assessment."

I knew the routine. No-Name showed me a whole bunch of pictures and I had to say what I saw. I sounded like a patient in a doctor's surgery when the doctor puts a stick in your mouth and asks you to say 'ah, eh, ee, oo, ou'. It was rubbish.

Test over, the Speech Therapist put her charts and books away and made to leave.

"You need to start using whole sentences, Harriet. Practise. That's the only way to improve."

"Is that it?" asked Charlotte, getting up and positioning herself in front of the door.

"Yes, that's it for today. You can go back to your lessons. I'll be back next term."

"But... it's not enough!"

I was shocked. What was Charlotte saying?

"And – sorry – who are you?"

"I'm just a friend," said Charlotte, her gaze falling to the floor.

"The thing is, it's up to Harriet. The ball's in her court, as they say. She needs to practise. That's the only way she will improve her speech."

"But, that's just it. She doesn't."

169

"Precisely. Now if you don't mind, I have to get to another school."

Charlotte opened the door and allowed the Speech Therapist to pass.

I caught hold of Charlotte's arm and looked into her eyes. *Drop it.*

But Charlotte was determined. "This can't be right. I'm sorry, Miss," she said, following the Speech Therapist into reception where she was signing out. "There must be something else you can do."

"And what do you suggest?" said No-Name, heaving her bag up onto her shoulder.

"I don't know... It's just she has so much to say and – well, it's like she's scared of using her voice."

"That's why she needs to practise," said the Speech Therapist, her voice finally softening.

"But she can't practise with just anyone."

What was she trying to do?

"What do you mean? Why not?"

"Well. There are some people she might be able to practise with... if she feels comfortable with them... but there are other people, who she doesn't know so well... and... well, it doesn't mean she doesn't have anything to say."

"And what should be done?" No-Name was starting to look interested for the first time since 11.30.

"Well I don't know. We've been using my spellchecker but it's a bit fiddly. And she's great with emails. Oh, I don't know. Isn't there something..."

"Do you know, I think I'm beginning to understand what you mean?" said the Speech Therapist.

What an idiotic woman, I thought.

"Would it be helpful, Harriet, if I could sort out a communication device for you? It would either talk for you, or it could be more like the spellchecker."

Yes – do such things exist?

"Well... I'll need to refer you to my colleague... and check out funding... we'll need to speak to your parents and see what they think. It will take some organising and there are no promises."

"Yes!!" mouthed Charlotte and put both her thumbs up behind the stupid woman's back.

"But you still need to practise your speaking," was the Therapist's parting shot.

"I will," I said, overcome with excitement. Why had no one thought of this before? Charlotte was amazing.

As soon as the door closed Charlotte thrust her hand forward.

"Hi five!" she said.

"Thanks," I said when we had finished celebrating.

"Let's just hope she does something about it," said Charlotte with a hint of doubt in her voice.

We passed Basil on the way to Geography. He tipped his cap.

"Your brother better today?" he asked.

"Yeah," I said.

Charlotte gave me the thumbs up sign for using my voice.

"Good," Basil called back along the corridor. "I don't want the job of cleaning up his breakfast again in a hurry."

*

That afternoon Mrs White accosted me in English.

"Is Jake Harris your brother?"

I nodded.

"Has he gone home sick again? Only he wasn't in registration this afternoon."

I shrugged. How would I know?

Chapter 33

Gloria had just finished helping with my Maths homework when the key turned in the front door and Jake poked his head into the kitchen.

"Hello, there, love. Fancy a cuppa?"

"Yes, please, Gloria. Hasn't it been a wonderful day? The daffodils are just glowing, like they're making their own sunshine, did you see it?" said Jake in a dreamy voice as he plonked himself down at the kitchen table.

What was he talking about?

He was quiet for a while, an insane smile on his face.

If Jake wasn't going to ask, and it didn't look likely from the way he was gazing in wrapped amazement at the kitchen sink, then it was up to me.

"How's Mum?" I tried to use my clearest voice.

"Well..." Gloria put a steaming mug in front of Jake. She looked reluctant to continue. "There was a bit of a set-back today. The hospital phoned up at nine o'clock for us to go and collect her. She was coming home. But, by the time we got there..."

"Yes?" I said.

Gloria sipped her tea.

"She had started to go into labour."

I couldn't breathe.

"Don't panic. They managed to stabilise her."

There was a long silence. Jake was gazing at the pattern on his mug. I wasn't sure if he had been listening. But he finally spoke.

"So, she's not coming home?"

"No, Jake, not yet. I'm sorry." Gloria put her hand on his hand which he had made into a fist on the table. He didn't pull away, just continued staring at his cup.

We finished our tea without speaking again. Then Gloria ousted us from the kitchen.

"Off you go, dears, unless either of you wants to set the table?"

Jake followed me into my bedroom.

"Hey!" he said, as if suddenly snapping out of a dream. "How come you've got the drums in here?"

"Gloria," I said. What planet had he been on? They weren't exactly quiet.

"Let's have a go," he said, pulling the stool out from the corner of the room and taking up the sticks. "Listen to the professional!"

He bashed out a sequence ending in a loud roll and a cymbal crash. He wasn't bad.

"On second thoughts," said Jake, chucking the sticks on the bed, "that's a killer for my head cramp."

He sat there looking as though he was waiting for me to speak.

"What's up?" I asked.

"What d'you think? I don't want to talk about it." He rubbed his head. At that moment, I could see what he'd look like in ten years' time... he looked so old.

"You at school today?"

"What?"

"You at school today?" I repeated, trying hard to articulate more clearly and signing so he could follow me.

"Yeah."

"All day?"

"Get off my case, right." He stood up abruptly.

"But Mrs White said..."

"Mind your own business, you." He pushed past, knocking the high-hat from the drum kit onto the floor with a loud crash.

The front door slammed as he went out.

"Is that Jake gone again?" Alan shouted from the living room.

Gloria's shoes hurried into the hall from the kitchen.

"Leave it, sweet pea. He'll come round. I just told him about Liz." She came into my room. "Dinner's ready, love. Come and get it."

After dinner, I checked my emails. At last I had a reply from Auntie Wendy. Her computer had been out of action and how was Mum and how were things going with Gloria? I replied:

Actually, Gloria's OK. We went into town on Saturday and I had my hair cut. It looks so cool. And we went to the beach and, you'll never believe it, we saw a whale!!
We went to see Mum too. She looked so small and lost with all the wires and tubes everywhere, but my friend says they're just monitoring the baby. And Gloria said that she went into labour today but that everything is stable again. Because of that she can't come home yet.
Will we still be able to come and see you in the summer?
Harriet

When Gloria came in to help me get ready for bed, I decided I would have to speak to her.

"I'm worried," I said.

"What's that?" said Gloria sitting down on the bed.

"Worried."

"Sorry, love. Say it again."

I picked up a felt tip and a sheet of paper from the desk. My writing was so babyish, but I tried my best, using capital letters –

'WORRIED', I wrote. The red ink looked like blood against the crisp white of the paper.

Gloria took the paper and screwed up her eyes.

"You're worried?" she said. "About your Mum?"

"Yes, and Ake."

"Jake'll be OK. He's just scared, that's all – for your Mum... for the new baby... for you as well, I expect. We're all worried, but Jake is at a difficult age anyway. I know it's tough for him and it's no wonder he's going off the rails a bit... it's a natural reaction..." she looked thoughtful. "You see. I recognise all the signs... it happened to me. I went a bit haywire... like Jake is now."

I willed her to go on.

"Your grandfather..." Her voice quivered.

I put my hand on Gloria's knee. I had always wondered about my real grandfather.

"He was such a good man... I did love him so..." She took a deep breath. "Well... He was killed in an accident. He was in the Air Force, you see. It was a routine flying mission. And no one knows why, but his plane just dropped out of the sky. And that was it, he was gone. It happened about a month before your Dad was born... and he had been looking forward to having a baby for such a long time..."

Gloria's obvious distress at telling the story made me want to cry.

"So, anyway. My whole life was turned upside-down. My husband gone; my home gone because we'd been living in married quarters... everything gone. Just like that. Believe me. Jake could get a whole lot worse. He just needs his space. He needs to be with his friends. He's probably doing the right thing."

More than anything in the world, I wanted to be able to get out of my chair and put my arms around her and just hold her.

*

I woke up when I heard the front door. It was eleven-thirty!

"That you, Jake?" called Alan in a sleepy voice.

"No, it's a burglar. You stupid old fool," Jake shouted, going upstairs. He went into the shower room then clattered about in his bedroom. After a time, he came back down to the kitchen.

As I dozed off, I distinctly heard the click of the front door again.

Chapter 34

I woke with a jolt in the early hours. It felt as though my hair was standing on end.

That dream again. This time I saw it happen. In slow motion. Jake at Bishop's Post in the storm in the wheelchair. Pushing forward the knob. Propelling himself towards the precipice. I tried to warn him, call him back, but my voice was drowned by the thunder. The front wheel went over the edge and the chair came to a precarious standstill. I thought he could still be saved, but to my horror, he leaned forward, tipping the balance. Chair and boy tumbled spinning into the water. They bobbed on the surface for a moment and then disappeared from view as though dragged down by an unseen hand.

I took a deep breath. It was only a dream. But where was he? What was he doing? I tried to go back to sleep but for a long time I could only doze and fret.

*

I jerked awake as a bolt of light hit my face. Was that him? But it was only Gloria opening the curtains.

"Up, up, up! Bright sunny morning, let's get moving. We're late; we've got some catching up to do – can we get you sorted in half an hour? I bet we can. We'll get you dressed before breakfast. Come on, we can do it."

Where does she get her energy from?

"Here's your things. You make a start, dear. I'll go and rouse your brother."

I was almost done when Gloria teetered back into the room. Even by Gloria's standards those heels were high.

"Will wonders ever cease? Your brother's already up and out. He's even had his breakfast – used up most of the milk in fact. Here, let's straighten you up," she said doing up my buttons and tie and pulling my seams into place.

Chapter 35

I had been looking out for Jake all morning at school. But there was no sign of him. Admittedly I didn't always see him but... Charlotte and I had eaten lunch together and were on the way back to the form room. I tugged on Charlotte's bag.

"What is it?" asked Charlotte.

"Spellchecker?" I said.

"What? It's in my bag... wait a mo." She dragged it out of a side pocket.

'can we go to the english room' I typed.

"Why?"

"Ake," I said.

"Jake? Your brother?"

Yes.

"What about him?"

'i think he stayed out last night' I typed.

"You what? What's he up to? Girlfriend?"

I shook my head slowly. *I don't think so.*

"What then?"

Don't know, I shrugged. I didn't like to think.

"OK," said Charlotte, leading me back to the lift. "So why are we going to the English room?"

181

'see if he's in school' I wrote.

"Oh, right, that's his form room."

Yes.

There was no sign of Jake in English One – or Cameron, for that matter, but Andy was talking to some of the girls over by the window. Some of the chairs had been kicked around the room a bit and Charlotte moved them out of the way, clearing a path for me. Andy looked up.

"Hi, Harriet," he said.

"Hi."

"What can I do for you?"

"Is Ake here today?"

"Err Jake?" said Andy looking at Charlotte.

"Yes, Harriet's worried about him. Is he in today?"

"No, he hasn't been around much all week. But I don't know… He's not walking to school with me anymore. He's gone a bit… off in the last few weeks."

I nodded slowly. *Thanks.*

"And Cameron…?"

Andy looked at Charlotte again for clarification, but Charlotte didn't know what I was saying.

"Use that," she said, pointing at the spellchecker which had fallen down the side of the chair.

'where does cameron live' I typed.

"Cameron McCarthy? He's on Elmtree Road, near the Rec. Aaron," he called across the room.

A tough looking boy with a number one haircut looked up.

"What number's Cameron's house?"

"Sixty-two, I think. Load of broken bikes outside. Who wants to know – Oi, wot you telling 'er for?"

"Listen," said Charlotte at home time, putting a piece of paper in my hand. "I've written out my mobile number and Messenger address. I don't know if there's anything I can do but send me a text if you want to talk… if you text me, I'll get on the Net. You have got Messenger on your computer?"

I nodded. I sometimes used it to talk to dad when he was away. It was easier than talking on the phone. I folded the paper and put it in my pocket.

Chapter 36

"How's your mum getting on, Harriet?" said the Warthog through the open window of the car as Sam pulled up on the drive that evening. She reached her arm round behind her to scratch her ample bottom as if I wouldn't notice.

I ignored her. I really wasn't up to one of the Warthog's lectures this afternoon.

She ploughed on. She had a bee in her bonnet, and nothing would stop her from blurting it out. "Haven't seen much of your Jake – except after the hours of darkness. Like I said to your grandmother, he shouldn't be in and out at all hours like that."

"Yes, and like I said to you, Mrs Turner," said Gloria, emerging from the back garden, her finger waggling and a stormy look on her face. "You should mind your own business."

"Oh! Oh!" said the Warthog, turning her back in a hurry and retreating to her house as fast as her stubby, gout-ridden legs would carry her. "I'm sorry, I'm sure. I'm just concerned is all. And I really don't care to be spoken to in such a manner. I don't deserve it…"

Her bee came back to sting her, I thought, grinning at Gloria.

"You seen Ake?" I asked as Sam drove off.

"No dear, stop worrying. He's never home before you. He'll be back sooner or later. Let's get you a hot drink. This sun's lovely, but it isn't warm."

The kitchen was full of the mouth-watering smell of baking. Gloria put the milk on the stove and took a tray out of the oven.

"I baked some bickies today. Biscuits out of a packet aren't a patch on the real thing."

I had to agree.

"Have you got homework for tomorrow?"

No.

"Good, we'll have a break from work then. I'm going to bring these things through on a tray. You can come and watch TV with me. I don't want you sitting in your room all night, brooding."

OK.

"All ready," she announced. "You go through first. We can watch whatever we like, your choice – Alan's down the betting shop. He'll probably go for a pint with his mate afterwards, so he won't be back for a bit." She put the tray down on the coffee table, switched on the TV and passed me the remote. "He's a silly old blighter, Alan, you know. Never wins, but off he trots every Wednesday and Saturday, like it's his religion. Crazy fool. That's men for you, dear."

*

Gloria's chicken casserole smelt good, but I wasn't concentrating on my food. Gloria and Alan were gossiping, Alan about the biddies at the bookies, Gloria about the OAPs at the gym – quite a cultural gathering, it seemed. But all I could really hear were the minutes ticking by on the clock. Why wasn't he home? Where had he been last night?

*

After dinner, I asked to use the phone.

"Of course, love," said Gloria looking surprised. "Who are you calling – one of your friends?"

I nodded.

I took the phone to my room and looked up Jake's mobile number. I dialled, my heart thumping. What would I say to him? I just wanted to know that he was all right.

"This person's phone is switched off. We will send them a message, by text, to let them know you have called."

I put the battery of my chair on to charge.

Chapter 37

Inane laughter emanated from the television set in the living room. The sound was up way too loud. Alan was snoring in Dad's armchair and Gloria looked as though she was also struggling to stay awake. Gloria really should consider the toll the gym was taking on her body. She was way too old for it.

The normally gentle hum of the wheelchair sounded like the roar of a Harrier Jet taking off. My heart barely dared to beat as I slid my coat silently from the banister. Alan's mobile phone lay on the hall table. I hesitated for a moment and then stuffed it into my blazer pocket. I opened the front door and sneaked out, closing it as quietly as possible behind me. The security light came on. I looked nervously at the Warthog's house, expecting the twitching of curtains at any moment. At the bottom of the drive I glanced into Mrs Turner's front room. Through the crack in the curtain I could clearly see her fat figure crammed into a chair in front of the TV, head tilted back, mouth wide open. So far so good. I pressed the knob of the chair forward anxious to be out of sight of the house. Once I was round the corner I stopped and put on my coat but I couldn't zip it up, instead I pulled the blanket up higher around my tummy to keep warm. I couldn't believe I was doing this.

It was a cloudless night and the stars were beginning to come out. A light breeze jangled a wind chime in the garden of number 17. I had never been out on my own before, even in the daytime, but I concentrated on keeping that concern from my mind. Elmtree Road was at least half a mile away. I had no idea how long it would take. Not wanting to be picked up and taken home by the police, I had decided to keep away from the main roads as far as possible, so I turned down a side alley. The streetlamp flickered, threatening to extinguish itself. I saw shadows that weren't there. Taking deep breaths steadied my nerves.

Each time I came to cross a road I had to detour to find the slopes in the curb which I could negotiate in the wheelchair. Once or twice, I found myself in the middle of the road searching for a way back onto the footpath. Fortunately, the streets were quiet, just the occasional car purring past.

A burly-looking man approached, walking an enormous Alsatian. They stepped out into the road to give me space. The man looked as though he was about to question me, but the dog suddenly strained at its lead trying to get to my wheels. It let out a volley of deep barks.

I jumped and willed my chair to go faster. My heart pounded even louder in my chest.

I turned a corner and stopped. All down the narrow pavement in front of me, green wheelie bins sat like an army of soldiers barring my way. It must be bin day in this neighbourhood tomorrow. Wracking my brain, I tried to rethink my route. If I went back the way I had come, onto Locksford Road, there was no pavement at all further down, but somehow, I would have to get onto the main road. If I could just get fifty metres down this road and turn left, I would be at the Rec. I approached the first bin but there was no way could I get past. I reversed the chair. Looking both ways I went down the dip and onto the road. The pavement on the other side was even narrower. No chance! I would just have to go down the middle of the road. A car came round the corner and blinded me. The driver came to an abrupt halt and jammed on his horn. I moved out of the way, behind a parked car.

"Get out of the road, you stupid idiot!" yelled the driver, his tyres screeching as he sped away.

I put my hands against my forehead, my whole body shaking. What was I doing? I was crumbling. Should I give up and go home? But I was well over halfway to Cameron's house – and when I found Jake he'd walk home with me. I waited for the trembling to subside then steeled myself and pushed the black knob forward. If another car came along, I would have to hide between the parked cars again. Simple. I wished it *was* simple. My throat hurt with the tension and my heart banged louder and louder. At the last parked car, a BMW convertible drove towards me, but it had seen me and was going slowly. It was driven by a little old man in a denim jacket and peaked New York cap. He leaned right forward in his seat, trying to see me properly, his big wiry eyebrows knitted in disbelief. He was shaking his head as he crawled past.

The Rec was an open stretch of common land. I just had to get through this, past the park, over the bridge and I'd be on Elmtree Road. I pulled the blanket round tighter. My joints were aching badly from the cold and the tension as though a sadistic physio had made me spend the day at Gloria's gym.

There was a path straight through the middle of the common which would be the quickest way. But it would look odd. A young girl trundling along, in the dark, at half past eight – *in a wheelchair!* I couldn't afford to draw attention to myself. Instead I took the path that led around the edge of the green. The hedge loomed dark and menacing at my side. It could hide no end of danger. I tried not to focus on what could be in there, but my eyes glimpsed dozens of pairs of big yellow saucers shinning out of the gloom. Watching me.

They're not real. They won't come out, I told myself.

I was relieved to get onto the main road. There was more traffic, but I felt closer to civilisation. Some of the cars seemed to be slowing down as they passed, but no one stopped. I imagined their occupants all on the phone to the police – "There's a girl out on her own in a wheelchair." Like you'd tell the police there was a dog running loose on the road.

On the opposite side of the street the big trees of the park creaked as the wind got up. It had got much colder all of a sudden. My wrists and ankles felt as though they were being repeatedly stabbed with icicles. I buried my left hand in the blanket.

I had to cross the main road at the crossing. I pushed the button and waited for the green man. The air felt wetter here and I could smell the river. The lights stopped the cars and I crossed. A man with a dog collar and a kind face stuck his head out of the window of his Fiesta.

"Are you OK?" he asked.

I nodded and tried to smile, to look as if it was normal for me to be out on my own at night. I reached the other side of the road and went over the bridge. The vicar drove slowly past. I gave him a wave and a smile, hoping that would satisfy him. I was relieved when he sped away, but I was certain *he* would be speaking to the police as soon as he got home.

I turned right into Elmtree Road. I was beginning to feel as though my feet would fall off with the cold. Leaning forwards, I tucked the blanket more tightly around my legs. I was nearly there. The house numbers on this side were all even numbers so I didn't need to cross the road.

The Elmtree Estate was full of young families. Pushchairs. The pavements had been built with family housing in mind. They were wider, smoother and easier to navigate.

There was a line of local shops on my side of the road. As I approached the bright lights felt welcoming but then the off-licence door opened, and a gang of youths tumbled boisterously onto the pavement. I hid behind an overgrown hedge and peered out. Was Jake there? I didn't recognise any of them. I listened to their conversation, laddish and bored. One thing was certain. They were looking for action. I knew I wouldn't get past them unscathed. I waited for a while, but it looked as if they had no intention of moving. I was outside number 38. Cameron's house would be well past the shops. To my right there was an alley. It probably went to a back access and ran along parallel to the main road and behind the shops. I had no choice. So, moving out of my hiding place I slipped into the narrow alley. It was unlit. I hesitated, but only for a moment.

I pushed forward, more slowly now. The alley did indeed lead to a pedestrian access that ran behind the houses and shops. It was very quiet. Only the empty laughter and shouts of the gang carried in the wind. My eyes slowly adjusted to the dim light.

The wheelie-bins behind the shops were overflowing. There was a scrabbling noise and I slowed right down. A fox looked up from its evening meal, just a few feet from my chair. Its eyes flashed green in the moonlight and it regarded me with interest but seemed frozen to the spot. I stopped and held its gaze. At last the fox blinked, turned and fled into a nearby garden, its tail streaming behind it. If I had been told, a fortnight ago, that I would meet a fox in a dark alleyway, on my own and half-way across town, I would have thought it impossible.

Once I was past the shops, I took the next alleyway that led back to the main road. I emerged at number 56. Nearly there.

Aaron was right about the bicycles. Most of the other houses on the street had tidy little gravel gardens with garden gnomes sporting goofy grins or fake water pumps. But number 62 looked distinctly shabby.

This was it. I hoped Jake was there.

Chapter 38

The house was as shabby as the garden and the glass in the door was cracked. The doorbell was too high to reach from the chair, so I knocked on the letterbox and waited. The lights were on and the shadow of a man moved away from the door. I leaned further forward and banged louder.

The shadow approached, swearing that it had stubbed its toe. A man opened the door slowly. He had greased down hair and a dark line of stubble. There was a strong smell of whiskey.

"Eh!" he said, looking down at me in surprise.

"Mr McCarthy?"

"Eh, Our Angela! There's a wee spastic girl on the doorstep in a wheelchair!" he called.

"Gee over, Jimmy," came a voice from inside. "You're seeing things again."

"No. Really, Angela. On our Cameron's life!"

"Aye and my brother's the Pope, you blithering fool. Get in here. Where's ma suppa?"

Mr McCarthy gave me an uncertain look as though he thought his wife must be right and I was only a figment of his imagination. He closed the door and his shadow could be seen staggering back up the corridor.

I gazed at the chipped blue paint of the door. Cameron's dad must be so used to hallucinating from overindulgence in the bottle that he almost expected it. It might have been funny if my situation wasn't so helpless. I hadn't come all this way for a drunken wally to think that I was an illusion.

I banged on the door again. But there was still no reply.

"Ah tell you, Angela..."

"Listen te me Jimmy McCarthy. There is no wee cripple at the door!"

I banged again, much harder this time.

"Sit doon, I tell you! Next there'll be fairies."

I looked around in exasperation. Was there a stick in this mess of a garden? I found the broken handle of a broom leaning up against the house. Angela couldn't deny my existence if I rang the doorbell.

The broom handle clattered about on the door as I tried to steady it against the bell. It rang. I held it down for so long that my presence there could no longer be in dispute.

"A'm coming, A'm coming!" shouted Jimmy. "Oh kay, oh kay!" he said, flinging open the door. "What is it?"

"Is Cameron here?"

"What's that you say?" He eyed the broken broom handle as if he thought I was going to use it to hit him. Which might have knocked some sense into him.

"Cameron."

"Our Cameron!" he yelled. "Cam-er-on." He stumbled to the bottom of the stairs. "Cameron! A visitor."

Mr McCarthy scratched his eyebrow as though he had never seen a stranger sight in his life.

"Ah told you, Angela..." he said, going into the living room.

Cameron came thumping down the stair looking worse than his father. His eyes were huge oceans and he looked around me rather than at me.

"What d'you want?" he slurred.

"Where's Ake?"

Cameron was holding the doorframe and lurching from side to side. I was afraid he was going to fall.

"Whey!" he said. "Have you seen the stars?"

"Where's Ake?" I repeated. I was getting angry – and increasingly alarmed.

"Jake?" said Cameron as though someone was dragging him away from an exotic dream. "Er – I dunno we was in the park. I... came on home... I think Jake went home too. But... well... he were loaded... unreal... Hey..."

196

But I was already reversing out of the garden. I had no idea what Cameron was talking about except that Jake might be in the park. I felt sick, hoping that Jake was in a better state than Cameron. But then Cameron had made it home. Jake hadn't.

Chapter 39

Four white pillars stood guard at the gates to the park like ghostly sentinels. Between them hung three gates, all locked with heavy padlocks. Jake's bag leant against the bars. On the inside. The wind whistled and groaned in the arching, leafless branches of the trees.

As far as I knew there was only this one entrance to the park. I drove all the way around the perimeter, calling out his name. The hedge was like a prison wall, keeping him in and me firmly out. I passed the children's area, where so many years ago we had laughed and played, safe and secure with mum. It was different now – more equipment, new paintwork, ultra-safe rubber surface. The playground stood empty; all its happy children tucked up safely in bed. One swing rocked absently in the wind as though an unseen mother was pushing her ghost child.

I was almost back at the main gate when I saw him through a gap in the hedge. On a bench next to the pavilion was a figure, slumped forward, its arms hanging by its side like a rag doll. Time seemed to slow down. I could no longer hear the wind; my body had frozen beyond feeling and my head was spinning. It was him. I was sure of it. I filled my lungs.

"Ja-ake!" I yelled as I had never yelled before. I felt my voice grow wings and float above me as though it had taken on visible form. I watched it pass through the gap in the hedge, across the path and over the grass. It funnelled into his ear. The figure on the bench raised an arm limply, as though a puppeteer was trying to make his doll wave, and then fell still again.

What could I do? I was so near and yet at the same time so far. Suddenly, the figure on the bench lurched. It seemed to go into spasm and threw up on the grass below. I caught sight of his face. It was definitely Jake. He slithered off the bench and into the vomit which steamed in the cold air.

I threw aside my blanket and leaving my wheelchair behind, lunged into the gap in the hedge. I hit my shin on the retaining wall. The spiky branches clutched at my clothing. They held fast to my coat so that I fell face first into the muddy soil and leaf-litter of the hedge undergrowth, my arms suspended behind me. My nose smashed on a rock and started to bleed; the pain blinded me for a moment.

My right arm came out of its sleeve quite easily and I heaved myself forward until my left arm followed. I went up on my elbows and pulled with all my might, trailing my useless legs. A sharp stone ripped into my stomach as I crossed the path. I did not care. My eyes were on Jake as I inched forward. Another convulsion wracked his body. I had to get to him. My arms were flooded with an energy I had never known, and I dragged and pulled myself over the grass. It was probably only a few minutes before I was by his side, but it seemed to take forever.

By the time I reached him he was still. Face down in the vomit.

With an enormous effort, I turned him over. He was covered in brown slime. I wiped the sick from his mouth and nose with the cuff of my blazer. My nose dripped blood on his best hoody. He groaned and I could have wept.

"Jake, Jake," I said, but he would not rouse. I pushed myself up on my left elbow and tried to balance while I got Alan's mobile out of my blazer pocket. But my shoulder gave way and I rolled down beside my brother, my hair in the vomit. The smell turned my stomach, but I ignored it.

"Emergency services, which service do you require?" came the young woman's voice.

"A..." I tried. "A..."

"Caller?"

I took some deep breaths. My throat felt as though lead balloons had blown up inside it.

"A..."

"Where are you, caller?"

"P… P…" Anger steamed inside me. "PARK." I shouted.

"OK caller, you're in the park. Which town? You've come through to the Aberdeen office."

I nearly threw the phone away in disbelief. Scotland?! I was a million miles away from Aberdeen.

"Caller?" came the voice.

I hung up in utter frustration and disgust. I called my home number, but it was engaged.

I lifted myself up off the ground and shook Jake. He groaned but there was no further movement.

I collapsed on his chest, hurting everywhere. Blood from my stomach had seeped through my torn blouse. Lifting it up I saw that there was a deep cut just above my tummy button. Then I remembered that Charlotte's number was in my pocket.

I typed a message into the mobile: HELP! AT PARK OPOSITE ELMTREE ROAD. NEED AMBULANCE NOW. HARRIET.

I sent; fingers crossed.

The phone rang within seconds.

"Harriet. It's Charlotte. I got your message – I was just thinking about you…"

I burst into tears.

"What's happened? Have you found Jake?"

"Ye-yes."

"Is he OK?"

"No."

"Dad's phoning an ambulance for you. What's wrong with him?"

I looked at Jake's face. He looked as though he was sleeping.

"Un…con…scious."

"Really! What about you? Are you all right?"

I looked at my torn clothes, the blood. I felt the numb fire of my frozen muscles and joints.

"Sort of…"

"Look, I'm getting dressed right now. Dad's going to drive over. It won't take long to get there; we'll be there in ten minutes."

Charlotte stayed on the phone, talking. I gripped the phone like a lifeline. After what seemed forever, I heard the howl of the sirens approaching and the trees of the park lit up with pulsing blue lights. And Charlotte was at the gate, scrambling through the hedge. I sank my head onto Jake's chest and dropped the phone.

Chapter 40

The next few days passed in a blur of pain, sleep and analgesics. Jake and I were both taken to the hospital. Gloria and Alan turned up at some point looking haggard. I was treated in Casualty for minor injuries and exhaustion and told I was going up to the children's ward. The doctors wanted to take Jake to a different department after needles and drips had been stuck into him, but I kicked up such a fuss that they wheeled a second bed into one of the side rooms in the children's ward.

I woke up several times during the night, with nurses at Jake's bed, taking his pulse and blood pressure. I lay mute, praying that he was all right. That I had got to him in time.

Hours later, I opened my eyes to find Jake looking at me, awake at last. Gloria sat awkwardly, dozing in a hard chair in the corner of the room. She looked grey and old.

"Did I dream it? You said my name properly... in the park," Jake said, his voice all furry.

"I did... J-Jake," I said, concentrating hard.

Jake smiled and we drifted back to sleep, holding hands through the bars of our beds.

When I woke again, it was late afternoon. Jake opened his eyes and rubbed his face.

"OK?"

"I think so." His voice was hoarse and weak.

"What happened?"

"Everything went so fast... I got into some bad stuff."

A tear fell on my pillow.

"Don't think about it," he said his voice cracking. "It's all over now."

"Promise?"

"Oh Harriet! I promise... I'm so sorry."

Later on that evening when Gloria had gone home for a change of clothes, Mum came down from the maternity and neonatal ward with tears and hugs and chocolate. It was odd to see her in a wheelchair. Her ward sister only let her stay for twenty minutes.

"She could still have an abortion," I said when she had gone.

"An abortion?!" said Jake in horror.

"Why not?"

"That would be like a betrayal to you."

What do you mean?

204

"It would be like saying if she had known you would be disabled, she would have terminated you as well."

We said nothing for a long time.

"If it wasn't for you, Harriet, I don't think I'd be here today. I think that would have been it..."

The next day, we were allowed visitors. Alan came in for a short while; Charlotte came in with her dad; Sam had taken the day off work and he came in with Evette and the most enormous bunch of flowers I had ever seen. Some of Jake's friends came too, though notably not Cameron. The police came and even a reporter interviewed us.

Dad arrived early the next morning, straight from the airport, full of sorrow and apologies and took us home.

When I returned to Milton Comprehensive a week later it felt like a lifetime since I had been to school. The blossom was now blooming in the warm spring sunshine and the bushes were finally opening their buds.

Sam opened the doors of the minibus. I drove slowly down the ramp and looked up at those hundred huge windows.

"You fit?" smiled Sam.

I smiled a watery smile.

"Come here," said Sam and put his arms around me.

I laced my arms over his shoulder and smelt the wax in his hair.

"You're OK, Harry. Go get 'em girl."

*

All the way down the corridor, people were calling out to me... "Hey, Harriet!"; "Well done, Harriet"; "Saw you on TV"; "Respect man!". I looked at Charlotte in bewilderment.

"You were on local *and* national news. Didn't you know?" Charlotte smiled and rubbed my shoulder.

Charlotte held the form room door open. The class fell silent as I went in. Everyone turned. All watching me. As I took my place even Greg looked at me with reluctant admiration.

"Good job, Harriet," he said looking embarrassed. "They say he'd of died if you hadn't got the ambulance."

He didn't have to say that. It seemed like a kind of truce. I was saved from responding when Miss Jenkins walked into the room, beaming.

"Well, Harriet," she said. "Welcome back!"

The whole class broke into spontaneous applause.

∗

I looked into the most enormous mirror I had ever seen. The make-up artist had made my face sparkle with an intelligence it never usually showed, and I wore a new silk blouse in electric blue bought specially for the occasion. There was a rap on the door and there was Mum, her large stomach stretched into a white evening gown.

"Are you about ready?"

I nodded.

"I'll prop the door open for you. They want you backstage in five minutes."

Mum waddled in and kissed the top of my head.

"I am so proud of you." She gazed at my reflection. "You look... radiant. Look, I'm going to cry! Right, I have to go. We're in the second row... you really are amazing."

She was gone.

That song filtered into my mind again...

'I cannot hide from what I see,
A mirror never shows the real me.
Inside I laugh, inside I crave,
Inside I cry, inside I'm brave,
I am not what you believe,
Inside – I am me.'

I took one last look in the mirror and I knew that it didn't matter about my appearance on the outside. Now I was proud of myself on the inside.

I went out of my dressing room to meet the Duchess of Kent and receive my Champion Children's Award for Bravery.

*

I was in my chair beside Gloria. We leaned over the railing and watched the sun playing in the ripples of the Southern Ocean. It was pleasantly warm although it wasn't yet ten o'clock. Daren and Kirsten were squealing as Jake chased them up and down the promenade. We'd had a call from England that morning. Mum had given birth to a little boy – only three weeks early. Everything seemed fine but it was early days.

"Are you feeling OK about the baby?" Gloria asked.

Yes.

"You're not worried at all are you, dear?"

I shook my head.

"No?" But Gloria still looked concerned.

'What will be will be,' I typed on the new communication aid attached to my chair.

Gloria seemed satisfied with that response and we turned back to look at the sea which arched away from us into the distance.

"You know," said Gloria as she shifted her weight on her four-inch sandals. "You remember I told you about the time when your grandfather died just before your father was born?"

"Yes," I said.

"Well... one of the reasons we were so looking forward to having a baby was that I had already had two babies. They were both stillborn. And both girls. It was good that your dad was a boy... I don't ever regret having him. But I have always longed for a little girl to call my own. I just wanted a happy, healthy little girl to hold in my arms.

"I was thrilled when you were on the way. I was convinced you were going to be a girl." She turned to face me, leaning her back on the railing and reached out to hold both my hands. "I was so hurt when I found out how... how disabled you were... I wanted nothing to do with you. I'm ashamed to say it." There was a quiver in her voice and her words kept faltering. "I was wrong... I should still have taken the time to get to know you. I know that now... Now that I've spent time with you, I can see how special you are." She drew me into a hug. I hugged her back, tears rolling silently down my face. I nuzzled my head into my grandmother's shoulder.

Gloria pulled away at last.

"I love you," she said. "And now I finally have that little girl who will always be my own."

And I love you.

Gloria stood up and we both turned back to the sea. In the distance two jets of water shot into the air. A large blue whale and a small blue whale rose out of the ocean. Time slowed. Two grey curves against the shimmering surface. They smashed back down, tails hovering, then disappeared out of sight.

I put my hand in Gloria's and squeezed.

THE END

'Historical' Note

Today I baked a lemon cake to celebrate one of my grown-up children coming to stay. I stirred up the ingredients and had it in the oven in ten minutes. As the cake was cooking, the mouth-watering aroma wafting into the kitchen, I spooned lemon curd into some icing sugar to drizzle over the top. Within an hour, we were sharing a beautiful, light and fluffy treat together.

'*Speechless*' has taken rather longer to create. The idea first came to me in 2006, when I was at university. My daughter, who has Cerebral Palsy, was then in Primary School and I was grappling with a big decision: should she go to the local Secondary School or to a Special School, further away from town?

The first draft of '*Speechless*' was completed in 2007. At that time, Facebook was in its infancy. The Internet was mostly 'dial-up' – Wi-Fi sounded like Sci-Fi! Mobile phones seldom had internet access. Mobile networks were temperamental at best and it really was true that if you called 999 from a mobile, the operator could pick up in any office in the country and have no idea where you were calling from!

It's incredible how quickly the world of technology has moved on!

I wish I could have given you a slice of lemon drizzle cake today, but I am thrilled to have shared Harriet with you instead.

If you have enjoyed *'Speechless'* and you would like more information about what inspired me to write this book or resources to use in the classroom, please take a look at my website: www.katedarbishire.com.

Kate Darbishire x

About the Author

Kate Darbishire lives in Dorset with her partner, and the youngest of her five children. She also has a very large and very fluffy English Springer Spaniel called Fluster who will walk forever over the nearby hills and fields.

Kate studied Creative Writing and Education at Bath Spa University and has worked as a Teaching Assistant in Special Schools for nearly ten years. *Speechless* is her first novel.

Made in the USA
Las Vegas, NV
23 March 2021